Albert

The Perished Riders MC - Mafia Series

Nicola Jane

Albert: Copyright © 2023 by Nicola Jane. All rights are reserved. No part of this book may be used or reproduced in any manner without written permission from the author, except in the case of brief quotations used in articles or reviews. For information, contact the author.

Meet the Team

Cover Designer: Francessca Wingfield, Wingfield Designs

Editor: Rebecca Vazquez, Dark Syde Books

Proofreader: Jackie Ziegler, Dark Syde Books

Formatting: Nicola Miller

Disclaimer:

This book is a work of fiction. The names, characters, places, and incidents are all products of the author's imagination and are not to be construed as real. Any similarities are entirely coincidental.

Albert is the second book in the spin-off series from The Perished Riders MC, where he appears throughout their books as an associate of the club. Therefore, it can be read as a standalone.

Books in The Perished Riders series:

Prequel - Riding Home

Maverick

Scar

Grim

Ghost

Dice

Arthur

Albert

Spelling Note:

Please note, this author resides in the United Kingdom and is using British English. Therefore, some words may be viewed as incorrect or spelled incorrectly, however, they are not.

Trigger Warning

The material in this book may be viewed as offensive to some readers, including graphic language, sexual situations, murder, violence, and references to historical sexual assault. (The author **does not** go into great detail).

Also avoid if you are easily triggered by trivial matters, such as the use of certain words, or how a character behaves.

Contents

Playlist	IX
Chapter One	1
Chapter Two	13
Chapter Three	25
Chapter Four	42
Chapter Five	57
Chapter Six	69
Chapter Seven	83
Chapter Eight	95
Chapter Nine	111

Chapter Ten	131
Chapter Eleven	151
Chapter Twelve	170
Chapter Thirteen	188
Chapter Fourteen	206
Chapter Fifteen	220
Chapter Sixteen	239
Chapter Seventeen	256
Chapter Eighteen	274
About the Author	283
Social Media	284
Also By Nicola Jane	285

Playlist

Don't Blame Me – Taylor Swift
Anti-Hero – Taylor Swift
Made You Look – Meghan Trainor
CUFF IT – Beyoncé
You Know I'm No Good – Amy Winehouse
Helium – Sia
Bad Thing – Jesy Nelson
Hold On – Chord Overstreet
You Only Love Me – Rita Ora
Falling – Harry Styles
Stay – Rihanna ft. Mikky Ekko
Feels Like Home – Matt Johnson

Chapter One

ROSEY

The grass crunches under my boots as I make my way through the large cast iron gates. I weave through the eerily quiet church yard until I come to the gravestone, the reason I'm here. I lay the single red rose on the ground. It stands out against the dullness of the stone and almost makes it look pretty along with the twinkling frost.

It's too cold to sit down today, so I remain standing, staring down at the weeds growing up through the soil.

"I'm sure you haven't missed me," I say out loud. There's no one around, but if there's one thing I've learned from years of coming here, no one minds when you talk to the dead. Usually, it's saved for loved ones, but trust me, he's not a loved one. Not by anyone, least of all me.

"But, Eagle, I couldn't miss the opportunity to update you on all the wonderful things you're missing." Eagle, the man I've hated for most of my life, was the president of The Perished Riders MC when I was younger and my mum was a club whore. Back then, the club liked their whores, and they dripped off the members like gold. But Eagle wasn't entirely happy with using just my mum. His attention turned to me when I was in my late teenage years. He'd told me I should have been grateful, that having the attention of the club president was an honour. It didn't feel that way.

"Meli is so happy." I smile at the thought of my best friend and Eagle's daughter. "She and Arthur are practically joined. You never see one without the other. She plans on having his kids." I laugh. "Bet you're turning in there at the idea of your little princess with a gangster. You'd have had him killed." I try to kick the dirt under my foot, but it's solid from the frost.

"Everyone at the club is happy. Mama B is looking after us all. Who would have thought she'd be so kind after everything?" I sigh. "I'm training someone. He seems okay, and it'll mean I can take a break from . . . my career. I'm going to spend more time with Ollie. He's getting big now, and he asks a lot of questions. That's when he's talking to me because, let's face it, teenagers hate their parents, right?" My heart twists a little.

"And he hates me. He wants answers, and I don't want to give them to him. He knows about you, of course he does, but he doesn't know what really happened." I groan. "I fucking hate you, Eagle. More than I hate anyone. I sometimes pray you're not dead, just so I can kill you all over again. I picture creative ways to make you suffer. I thought that'd stop after I ended you."

"Mum?" I spin around and stare into the eyes of my twelve-year-old son, Ollie. No one knows about these visits except Dice, and especially not Ollie.

"Why are you here?" My question comes out harsher than it should.

"Why are you here?" he counters, arching a cocky brow.

"I'm the one asking questions," I snap. "You should be in school."

"Free period," he says, rolling his eyes.

"We're not in America, Ollie, you don't get free periods."

"Like you'd know," he scoffs, and my heart twists again. He likes to pull the shit parent card a lot.

"Let's go. I'll take you back to school," I mutter.

"Aren't we going to discuss this?" he asks, waving his hand around. "Why you're here, standing over Dad's grave? I thought you hated him."

"I do." I begin to walk away, hoping he'll follow and change the subject.

"Bullshit," he snaps, and I spin back to face him.

"Don't use that kind of language around me," I hiss. "You're twelve, it's not appropriate."

"I'll tell you what's not appropriate, you visiting Dad and not telling me about it. Do you come here a lot?"

I hesitate before shaking my head. "No," I lie.

"You were talking to him."

"I was singing," I snap.

"To Dad?" he asks, smirking.

"To myself. Just stop, Ollie, okay. Stop. You need to be back in school. I'll drive you."

We get back to the car, and I pull out onto the main road before he's had chance to get his seatbelt on. "I would have come with you," he mutters.

ALBERT

I grip the steering wheel tightly. "How long have you been coming here?" I ask.

"A while."

"You shouldn't."

"Why?"

"Because," I mutter, "it would upset Mav and Mama B."

"Until you all tell me why he's so hated, I'll continue to see him."

I sigh. "No, Ollie, you won't. I forbid you to."

He laughs, and I bite my tongue so I don't say something I can't take back. "Since when did you forbid me to do anything?"

I glance over at him, frowning. "I forbid you to do a lot of things. Like smoking, drinking, swearing."

"Mum, you're raising me in an MC, hardly a place you should want me to be if you don't want me to do all those things."

"Christ, are you doing those things?" I ask, realising I have no idea what he does when he's away from me.

"You'd know if you were around more."

I drive in through the school gates. "Well, that's going to happen soon enough. I'm reducing my hours at work so I can be home more."

He rolls his eyes and gets out of the car. "Go, before my teacher—" It's too late, his head teacher rushes out the door waving like a crazy witch. "Great," Ollie mutters.

"If this is about today, he had an appointment, I just forgot to tell you," I say as she leans into the car through the door Ollie exited.

"Actually, it's about Ollie's behaviour. I have tried to call you several times, and you haven't got back to me." I wince, remembering the voice messages. I had every intention of getting back to her . . . eventually.

"Right, sorry, I've had a lot on at work." I turn off the engine and get out the car. She closes the passenger door. "Ollie, go to class. We'll talk tonight," I add.

Once he's gone, I smile at Mrs. Ball. She's an odd-looking lady who dresses like she's in her eighties, but I have a sneaky suspicion she's a lot younger. "His behaviour?" I prompt.

"He's had several detentions, missed more lunchtimes than I care to remember, and he's not handing in any of his homework."

I nod. "I'll talk to him."

"And then he walked out of his lesson today without an explanation. Quite frankly, I'm sick of hearing his name from his teachers. He shows no respect for the staff or his classmates, and he's always in some kind of scrape with other boys his age. We're very concerned."

"Why don't you tell me what you'd like me to do?" I ask.

"I think we should work together to understand why he's behaving this way."

I sigh. "He's a typical boy, Mrs. Ball. It's a stage they go through."

She smiles awkwardly. "You don't need to tell me, I've been teaching them for almost twenty years."

"Look, let me speak to him tonight. I'll call you tomorrow, and we can discuss it."

She nods stiffly. "Okay, but I should warn you, this is his last chance. So, we'll need to work together quickly if Ollie wants to remain at this school."

Mav sits across the main room watching me. I try to ignore him, but eventually, he comes over to where I'm sitting on the couch. "Okay, spill."

"Huh?" I ask.

"You're not skipping around, and you haven't annoyed Dice once since you got back. He even walked past you extra slow to give you a chance. Something's wrong."

I contemplate not telling him. He hasn't exactly taken an active interest in Ollie, even though they're half-brothers. "Stuff with Ollie," I mutter.

He takes a seat. "Is he okay?"

"The school's on my back about his behaviour. He looks at me like he hates me. I'm having a parent guilt fest right now."

"Have you talked to Mama B?" he suggests.

I frown. "You want me to ask her for advice about her dead husband's secret love child?"

He smirks. "When you put it like that . . . but seriously, she's good at that sort of thing. She raised me, didn't she? And I don't think she struggles with you both like she did when you first returned." He's right, Mama B treats me the same as everyone else here, and she treats Ollie like she does her grandchildren.

"It's just hard sometimes, yah know. I still feel like a teenager myself most days, and I hate that we're not close like we used to be. Before I came here, it was just me and him against the world and it worked. Now, I'm lucky if he even looks in my direction."

"Isn't that just teenagers for you? They're all like it. I could speak to him for you, if you like. He doesn't usually backchat me." No one talks back to Mav—he's the club President.

"It's worth a try."

ALBERT

I stare wide-eyed at Archer. He's taking over from Rosey, and she's been showing him the ropes, but I have to admit, as much as she annoys the hell out of me, I prefer her way over Archer's. "What?" he asks innocently.

"It's not a clean kill," I say like he's stupid, which right now, I think he is.

"It's still a kill," he replies, shrugging.

"Arthur won't be happy," I mutter, looking around at the mess in the shop. We've been trying hard to pull ranks back on the streets after recently acquiring a new area. It's been run by street gangs for a long time, so getting on top of the thugs who think they still run those streets is a pain in the arse. It's a job we passed to Rosey and her sidekick, Archer. "Where is Rosey anyway?"

"Problems with her kid, apparently."

I shake my head in irritation. This is why we shouldn't hire people who are not one hundred percent invested. I throw Archer a burner phone. "Call the clean-up and get this sorted. I'll update Arthur, but he won't be happy."

My older brother, Arthur, lives in a newly built house right at back of the MC's clubhouse. Since he got with the President's sister, Meli, he's done everything in his power to make her happy, including moving her closer to her old home.

I spot Rosey outside the clubhouse, sitting on the wall, looking lost. I march over. "Where the fuck were you today?" I snap, bringing her from her daydream. "Archer caused a right mess, blood everywhere."

She inhales and releases it on a sigh. "I was busy."

"Busy?" I yell. "You let me down and you don't even have an excuse ready?"

She jumps off the wall. "I don't work for you, Albert. And right now, you're pissing me off," she snaps. "If Arthur's got a problem, tell him to put it in writing."

ALBERT

I grab her arm, pulling her to me. It's risky given her quick reflexes and short temper, but she doesn't react. Instead, she crashes against my chest, placing her palms against it and resting her head on her hands. I frown. She's acting odd. "Are you okay?"

"Don't be nice," she whispers. "Whatever you do, don't be fucking nice. It'll tip me over the edge."

I glance around to make sure we're alone before gently tucking her hair behind her ear. "Anything I can help with?"

She shakes her head. "Nope." She looks up into my eyes, and I see the sadness that's usually well hidden. "I should get back inside. I've left Mav to talk to Ollie. I couldn't be in there while Mav had his President head on. It makes me wanna jump in and defend the kid."

"Ollie's in trouble?"

She nods. "With school. Mav's pulling rank."

"If you're free later..." I begin, but she's already shaking her head. We've hooked up a couple times in secret, a no strings kind of deal, but if I ever try to arrange it, she always turns me down. It's on Rosey's terms completely, and I'm okay with that. "Well, the offer's there. I'll be at

Bertie's most of the night unless I get called out to help your protege."

She smiles. "Archer's not so bad."

I roll my eyes. "If you don't mind paying for an extra clean-up team every time he does a job."

Chapter Two

ROSEY

I tap lightly on Mav's office door, and he barks, "Come in," from inside. When I enter, Ollie looks to be in full-on sulk mode, and Mav looks ready to rip his hair out. "Everything okay?" I ask.

"Ollie's got something to say," Mav replies, glaring at my son.

"Sorry," he mutters, rolling his eyes.

"Boy, I know you didn't just roll your eyes," Mav roars, making both me and Ollie jump.

He sits straighter. "Mum, I'm sorry for my behaviour. I'll get it in check," he says, this time more genuinely. I nod. "Can I go now?" he asks, looking to Mav for direction.

Mav also nods, and he wastes no time escaping the office. I sit on the seat he vacated.

"Fuck, is this what I've got to look forward to?" Mav asks, flopping back in his chair.

I laugh. "It'll be worse with Ella. Girls are way worse than boys."

"Ella is bad enough already and she's only eight. Can I send her to boarding school?" he jokes. Ella is his stepdaughter, but you wouldn't know because they're both so comfortable around one another. She even calls him 'Dad'. And now, Rylee's given him a baby boy, Reuben.

"Did he give you a clue as to what's going on in his life right now?" I ask hopefully.

He shakes his head. "But honestly, I wouldn't worry. It's just teenage boys. He'll grow out of it."

I shouldn't take Albert up on his earlier offer. I know as I sign my name in the guest book it's a bad idea. But Ollie locked himself in his room, and Mama B gave me a lecture on making more time for him. I just felt the need to run, so here I am, standing at the bar of Bertie's. He refers to it as a prestigious club, but it's basically a strip bar that men pay a fortune to be a member of.

The barman smiles, recognising me instantly. "Cherry sours, right?" he asks. I smile, nodding. It's not the sort of drink they stocked here until I asked for it. He hands me the glass and adds, "I'll put it on Mr. Taylor's account."

"Have you seen him?" I ask.

"He was heading for the black room last time I saw. He might have a meeting," he says. I drop him a text.

Me: I'm here, at your bar, like you requested.

A few minutes pass before he replies.

Albert: I'm in a meeting. Hang around?

I scoff. I wait around for no one, and he should know that by now. I drink the sours and head across the bar with a confidence well practised. Men turn to look, and I feel their eyes taking in the sway of my arse in the tight leather skirt. I run my hands over the leather wrap that criss-crosses over my chest to make sure it's still hiding the important parts, then I gently shake out the roots of my hair and take a breath.

I push open the black doors. Albert looks up first, he's lounging in one of the large chairs surrounding a poker table. There are seven other men around the table, all with cards in their hands, a pile of poker chips in the centre of the table. I stand in the doorway with my arms folded and an arched brow. "Hang around?" I repeat, and Albert groans. "Like a fucking puppy dog?"

I close the door and head through the room to another door. This leads to a private room, which I enter and I begin to unwrap my top. I keep my eyes fixed on Albert, and the second he realises I'm about to undress, he rushes towards me, slamming the door closed and almost knocking me off my feet.

His kiss is urgent as he presses his hungry lips against mine. "Now, who's the fucking puppy dog?" he pants, pulling his shirt free of his trousers.

I smile against his mouth. "Good boy," I whisper.

I drop my top to the floor, and he steps back to admire my perky breasts. A groan escapes him. I reach beneath my skirt and pull my underwear down, expertly lifting one leg and freeing the lace garment. I hand it to Albert, and he presses it to his face, inhaling deeply.

He shakes his head, smirking. "Bend the fuck over and don't say another word."

I turn, bending slowly and touching my toes. "Yes, Sir," I tease.

ALBERT

His hand burns as he slaps me on the arse. "That was two words."

I hear his belt buckle opening and then his zipper. He tears a wrapper open, taking out the condom. I brace myself for his intrusion, and when it comes, I relax completely, letting him take control as he eases into me. Once he's fully inside me, he grabs a handful of my hair and pulls me to stand. I feel fuller, groaning in pleasure before he's even begun.

"Move," he orders. I think he gets a kick out of having the power, and right now, so do I. I press my hands against his thighs and begin to move against him. He stays still, and when I look back over my shoulder, he's staring down between us, a heated look on his face. "Touch yourself," he pants. I bring one hand between my legs, immediately feeling wetness there. He grips my hips impatiently and begins to move, slow at first, then picking up speed. I let my nails graze against his cock each time he pulls out, and he growls in pleasure. It's not long before I'm crying out. Albert clamps a hand over my mouth, grunting in my ear as he follows me over the edge.

He stills, his hand still over my mouth. The heavy sound of our breathing fills the room, and I get that feeling I always get after I do shit like this—I want to leave. I step away from him, pulling my skirt back into place, and then I pick my top off the floor and wrap it around, securing the zip at the back. Albert watches me, and I know he wants to say something but chooses wisely to stay quiet as I head for the door.

"You forgot something," he says. I glance back at him holding up my underwear.

"Keep them, a souvenir."

"I'd rather you put them on while you're out there, unless you're heading straight home?"

The way he says it, sounding hopeful, pisses me off. If I want to hang around with no knickers on, I'll do just that, so instead of answering him, I pull the door open and head back through the room where the poker game is still in play. "I hope you didn't peek at his cards, boys," I say as I pass.

"Do you play?" asks one.

I pause. "A little."

"We have enough players," snaps Albert, stepping into the room looking slightly less put together than he did before our little encounter. I smirk.

"We can deal her in. We're starting a new game," one of the men replies, pulling out a seat next to him.

Albert watches me in irritation because he already knows I'm going to agree. I nod once and head back over to the table, taking the offered seat. "Really?" asks Albert, glaring wide-eyed. "You wanna play with the big boys?"

I grin wider. "I've been playing with big boys since I was thirteen years old, Bert. Sit down and watch an expert." The men around the table laugh, and the one nearest to him slaps him on the back. I reach over to Albert's stack of chips. "I'm just gonna borrow these," I tell him, sliding them towards myself.

"Why do you always come here empty handed, Red?" he asks, arching a brow.

"I'm like the Queen, Albert. I don't carry cash."

I play the first couple of hands badly, luring them into a false sense of security. Albert groans each time I lose more of his money. He has no faith in me, but my mum taught me to play poker at six years old. When you're a club whore like she was, you have to know how to make money quick.

There's a good pile of chips on the table when I reveal a flush. The men around me groan, chucking their cards in, and I smile innocently. "I won?" I gasp.

"Beginner's luck," mutters the man next to me.

I lose the next hand, and they all relax a little.

ARTHUR

I can't keep my eyes off Rosey, knowing she's naked under that tiny skirt is driving me insane. I had her two hours ago and I want her all over again. We're on the last game and we've put all in. I need it to end, so I can get Rosey alone. Two of the guys have already folded and they're soon followed by the rest until it's just me and Rosey. Staring down at my cards, I have a good hand, and I'm more than confident I've got this in the bag. "I'm about to win," I tell Rosey. "Wanna make it interesting?"

"Go on," she says.

"If I win, you give me an entire night . . . tonight." The men make approving sounds.

"And if I win?" she asks.

I laugh. "Whatever you want, Red."

She thinks for a minute. "You take me on a date, no expense spared."

"You don't date," I say, "but sure, whatever." Her suggestion tells me she's not got the winning hand because she hates romance. She's not the type of girl you take home to meet your mother.

She smiles, laying her cards on the table. I lean over, hardly trusting my eyes. "Royal flush," she confirms. The men all lean closer too.

"Fuck," Jack whispers. "That's not beginner's luck."

I throw my straight flush on the table as Rosey sweeps the chips towards her. "I'll take cash, boys."

I remain seated as the men file out the room. Rosey sits opposite me, still looking smug. Once the door closes, I lean forward, resting my arms on the table. "Did you cheat?"

Her mouth falls open. "I resent that."

"A royal flush," I say. "Who the fuck is that lucky?"

"For my date, I was thinking a limo to pick me up, a drive around London while I sip Champagne, and dinner somewhere expensive. I really want to try lobster."

"Of course, you do," I say, rolling my eyes.

She stands, moving towards me. "And maybe, if you play your cards right," she laughs at her own pun, "I'll let you pay for an exclusive room in a top hotel where you can," she straddles me, taking my tie between her fingers, "taste every inch of me."

I feel my cock stir to life again. "You hate romance," I point out.

She rocks against me, and I close my eyes briefly, enjoying the feel of her heat pressed against me. "Who said anything about romance? A night out, no expense spared. I've never had that so . . ." She trails off and that look of sadness and confusion returns to her eyes. Maybe she didn't mean to say that out loud.

"Never?" I repeat. "You've never been on a date?" She shakes her head. "But you're what, thirty?"

She pushes herself up onto the table and places her feet either side of my thighs on the chair. "I'm not the kind of girl men date, Albert. We both know that." She runs her fingers along her legs, inching her skirt up slightly. "Now, do you want to talk about the many failings of my love life, or do you want to make me come with your tongue?" She lies back, opening her legs.

"Definitely option two," I mutter, burying my head between her thighs.

Rosey drinks the cherry sours in one go and places her glass on the bar before placing her mobile to her ear. "I'll be right down," she says, before disconnecting.

"I can take you," I offer.

She shakes her head. "No offence, but that's a bit weird. Before you know it, we'll be sharing a toothbrush in your bathroom."

I roll my eyes. "Hardly. Who's coming to get you?"

"Archer."

I stiffen. I don't know why it bothers me, it just does, but I can't show that, so I lead the way, saying, "I'll walk you out."

Before we step outside, I grab her hand and pull her behind a pillar. "That date," I say, "let's make it for tomorrow."

"I have a job on," she replies.

"With Archer?" I ask, unable to hide the annoyed tone of my voice.

She narrows her eyes. "Yes, obviously."

"I thought you were stepping away from the jobs to spend time with Ollie."

Her expression hardens and she pulls free. "Goodnight, Albert."

"We're going on the date, Red," I yell after her. "I always pay up on my debts."

Chapter Three

ROSEY

Watching Archer work is like watching a messy kid running around with paint. Only this isn't paint, it's blood . . . lots of blood. I wince as he hits a main artery and more crimson fluid sprays across the room.

I jump down off the bench I'd perched on. "I can't take it anymore," I announce, and he stops, looking over to me. "Why are you so messy?"

He shrugs. "I like blood."

"Save your kinks for the bedroom, Arch. The less I know about that, the better." I take the knife from him and examine it. "Has this ever been sharpened?"

"It gets the job done."

I groan. "How the hell haven't you been caught before?"

"Luck."

"Your luck will run out if you don't start listening to me."

He scoffs. "I've been doing this for a year."

"And I've been doing it since I was eighteen. Mr. Taylor isn't going to send you any work if he sees this sort of shit. He thinks I'm reckless, he's seen nothing yet."

"I get the job done. I don't see the problem."

"The problem, Archer, is the more mess there is, the more expense there is for the clean-up. That'll eventually come out of your part of the money because the Taylors are understanding, they know sometimes things get messy, but with you, it's every job." I look down at the dead body. "You cut into his artery."

"It's a quick death," he argues.

"It's a messy death. You'll get blood splatter on yourself, which ties you to this murder scene. You should do some research on the human body. Avoid all messy areas, especially arteries."

"Jesus fucking Christ," comes Albert's voice, and I sigh. "This is like an episode of *CSI*. What the hell happened?"

ALBERT

"My fault," I say before Archer can answer. "Sorry, I hit the artery by mistake."

He places his hands on his hips and stares back and forth between me and Archer. "Yet he's the one covered in blood. And you're reckless, Red, but not stupid. Get this cleaned up now and then burn the place to the ground."

"If we're burning it, why do we need to clean up?" asks Archer. I elbow him in the ribs, and he hisses, glaring at me.

"Because it's a fucking shitshow of DNA, you stupid prick. Rosey, outside, now," he snaps, disappearing back through the door. I follow, giving Archer one last glare. Albert's pacing. There's something hot about a powerful man looking stressed.

"He's still learning," I offer with a shrug.

"Learning?" he growls. "Ollie could do better than him. What the fuck do I do with a rookie who spills blood like it's a river? He's gotta go."

"Come on, he lost out on the cash from Jolene," I remind him. That's how I met Archer—one of Arthur Taylor's enemies had hired him to kill Albert and Meli.

Albert laughs. "If I'd have known that was what was coming for me, I wouldn't have worried."

"He might be messy, but he's good. He would have gotten you."

"Yeah, and spread me over half of London. I'd rather pay him *not* to work for us."

I smile. "Give him another chance. I promise I'll keep a closer eye on him, and I'll show him the way."

He stops in front of me. "That date—"

"It's a stupid idea," I begin. I don't even know why I said it. I was in the moment. "Forget about it."

"Tomorrow night."

"Albert, honestly, just forget I said anything."

"Do you want your sidekick to keep his job or not?"

"That's blackmail."

He grins. "I'm not a nice guy, what can I say?"

"Which is the exact reason a date isn't a good idea. Anyway, have you ever taken a woman on a date in your life?"

He shakes his head. "Nope. And you've never been on one, so let's learn together."

Archer comes out, and Albert gives him an irritated look. "Anyone got a match?" he asks.

My mobile rings and I see Ollie's name. He never calls me, so I answer right away. "Ollie?"

ALBERT

"Mum, can you come and get me? I need you." His words chill me.

"Of course, send me your location."

Albert is watching as I disconnect and check the map that Ollie sent through. I frown. "Do you know this?" I ask, showing him.

He looks concerned. "Why is he there?"

"Where is it?"

"I'll take you now."

I shake my head. "No, I'll find it, don't worry."

"Rosey, it's not safe. That area is in the middle of a gang war. I'll take you."

I hand Archer a box of matches and then follow Albert to his car.

We drive in silence for a few minutes before he finally repeats his question. "Why is he there?"

"I don't know, Albert. I don't know why he's there or who he's with. All I know is he must be in trouble if he called me over any of the MC."

"He's hiding it from Mav for a reason," he mutters, glancing my way. I thought the same, but I keep quiet. I don't know what Ollie's involved in, but it can't be anything good if he's on an estate owned by gangs.

Ollie waves us down. He's practically hiding behind a post, so Albert slams on the brakes, and I jump out the car, closely followed by Albert. "Are you okay?"

He nods, letting me run my hands over his face to check for marks. "Mum, I'm fine," he says, taking my hands and holding them in his. "But we have to go." I glance around, there's no one about.

"In the car," says Albert, and we get in. I twist around to face Ollie in the back. "Why are you here?" Albert asks.

"My friends wanted to go to a party here, but there was a massive fight, so everyone ran."

"And you know this area isn't safe, right?" I ask.

"I didn't, not until Ben mentioned it."

Once we get back to the clubhouse, Ollie gets out the car and heads inside. "Thanks," I say to Albert.

"Do you believe him?" he asks.

I nod. "Why wouldn't I?"

"Because he's a kid. He was in a bad part of town, and he was hiding when we found him. Come on, Rosey, something's not right."

"I'll deal with my son, don't worry. And don't mention this to anyone, especially not Maverick."

"Because you know I'm right."

ALBERT

"Because I don't need any more lectures about my child. He called me, Albert, that's a first. And I'm taking it as a win, so I'm not going to go too hard on him. I'm giving him the benefit of the doubt."

"It's a mistake. I see kids like Ollie getting involved in gangs all the time, and they don't get out once they're in."

"You see it because you're the ringleader," I snap, angry he's trying to tell me how to parent.

"Ouch. I'll send you the details for dinner tomorrow."

I scoff, getting out the car. "Don't bother. I'm going to be busy."

Ollie is already in his room, tapping away on his mobile. I go in, taking a seat on the edge of his bed, and he places his phone on his chest. It's never far from him.

"Please don't lie to me, Ollie. Are you in a gang?"

He laughs. "Don't be crazy."

"Because if you are, I can help. They tell you it's a family, but it's not true. They'll leave you the second shit goes down."

"Relax, Mum, I'm not in a gang."

I give a nod and try a different tactic. "I visit Eagle's grave sometimes. I don't know why. It's just peaceful there." I figure opening up might lure him to do the same.

"I was passing and saw your car. I haven't been before," he admits.

I brush his hair from his eyes, the way I used to when he was small. "For so long, it was just us. I didn't think how it would affect you when we moved in here and I started working more. I just saw that you were being taken care of."

"It's fine. You were doing what you needed to."

"Do you mean that?" I ask. "Because I feel like you hate me."

He smiles. "I'm supposed to act that way, you're my mum. But thanks for coming to pick me up tonight. Even if you did bring Albert." He picks his phone up again. "Are you and him . . ."

I shake my head. "God, no. Imagine having him as your stepdad."

He grins. "Yeah, imagine."

ALBERT

ALBERT

I went all out for this date, calling in a favour to get a table at an exclusive restaurant that specialises in lobster. I sent a driver to collect Rosey, and as I finish my first glass of whiskey and check my watch, my mobile rings. It's my driver. "She's not here, Mr. Taylor."

I frown. "What do you mean she's not there?"

"Maverick said she left half an hour ago and he's no idea where she went."

"Great," I mutter.

"He said she was quite drunk, and with Meli."

I disconnect and call my brother. "Arthur, where's Meli?"

"At home," he mutters. "I'm at the office. What's up?"

"She's not at home, she's with Rosey, and Rosey should be here with me."

I hear him sigh heavily. "Let me track her."

"Does she know you track her?" I ask, laughing.

"No, and don't you dare tell her. They're at Bertie's," he says. "I'll meet you there."

Arthur is outside Bertie's speaking with the door staff. I head over, shaking his hand and following him inside. "Thought Meli would be on a tighter leash, to be honest, brother," I say with a smirk.

"Let's not pretend I own her, Bert. We all know she runs rings around me, but that's half the fun."

Meli yelps in surprise when Arthur slides in behind her at the bar. He gently tugs her head back and whispers in her ear right as Rosey turns back to hand her a drink. She catches my eye before turning back to the barman. I don't know what game she's playing, but it's starting to piss me off. Arthur follows the women over to their table, but I decide to have a walk around the club. I'm regretting tracking her down and following her here like I'm her bitch.

Alex, my newest dancer, spots me, winking seductively and crawling across her stage towards me. I stop, letting her run her hand over my tie. "Mr. Taylor, can I dance for you?" I drop down into a seat and nod. Anything to take my mind off Rosey.

My body doesn't react to the dancers like it used to. Maybe I'm immune, but when I first opened this club five years ago, I was a walking hard-on. Now, as Alex does her best to seduce me, I'm unaffected, glancing over to

ALBERT

Rosey instead and wondering why she's so fucking cut off from the world. Alex finishes on a split, biting her lower lip and giving me a sexy smile. I don't usually pay for my own dances, but I pull out a tonne anyway and slide it towards her. She grins. "You're supposed to hook notes in my knickers as I dance."

"Yeah, well, that ain't my style."

I stand, and she swings her legs over the edge of the stage while hooking her arms into her bra. "What is your style?" she asks.

I frown, irritated by her chatter. "Huh?"

She jumps down and turns, indicating for me to fasten her bra. "Tell me what you like, and I'll accommodate." Usually, girls go out back to dress again, but I fasten her bra and she spins to face me, taking hold of my tie again. "I'm eager to please you," she whispers. Her eyes twinkle under the bright lights and her perfectly plump pink lips are natural, a rare sight these days. I pinch her chin gently between my thumb and finger, contemplating whether I should throw the rules out the window for one night and make use of the table I've got booked in just under an hour.

I sigh. "Tempting," I murmur. "Very tempting."

"But you've got other things on your mind?" comes Rosey's voice from behind me. I glance over my shoulder. "It's the best excuse without upsetting her."

"Who said I was going to upset her?" I ask, releasing Alex and turning to face Rosey.

She shrugs. "It sounded like you were about to let her down."

"You're the let-down among us," I point out. Reaching behind me, I find Alex's hand and tug her to stand beside me. "Have a good evening, Red."

"I'm disappointed," Rosey says, following us towards the backstage door.

I sigh. "Why's that?"

"I thought you'd fight harder," she muses, tipping her head to one side. "Turns out I was right." And then she spins on her heel and walks away.

"What was that about?" asks Alex, as I stare after Rosey. "Who is she?"

I shake my head, bringing myself back into the room. "What?"

"Is she an ex or something?"

I laugh. "No. I don't have an ex. Relationships aren't my thing." I drop her hand, and she's disappointed. "Thanks for the dance, Alex."

I'm in the office when Arthur comes in. "I'm taking Meli home," he announces.

"Okay. Catch you tomorrow?"

"What did you want Rosey for anyway?" he asks, and I look up at him blankly. "You said earlier she was supposed to be with you. How come?"

"Just a work thing."

"Anything I can help with?"

I shake my head. "No, I've got it all under control."

"I know she's a bit of a handful," he says, backing out the office, "but she's good at what she does."

I grin. "Don't let her hear you say that, she'll get a big head."

Half an hour passes, and I consider locking up the office and heading home when Rosey saunters in with a large paper bag. I eye her suspiciously as she locks the door and heads towards me. "Dinner," she says, holding the bag up.

I lean back in the chair, watching as she places the bag on the desk and proceeds to unpack the food. When she's done, she wipes her hands down her jeans. "What is this exactly?" I ask, exasperated by her behaviour.

"It's dinner," she says, dragging a chair from the edge of the room over to my desk and seating herself. "I got burgers because everyone loves a burger, and you don't look like a vegetarian, so I—" I hold my hand up to stop her talking, and she bites her lip. "You're not a veggie, are you?"

"I meant, why have you gotten us dinner?"

She frowns. "I thought you might be hungry."

I pinch the bridge of my nose. "I booked us dinner, remember?"

"I told you not to," she mutters.

I slam my hands on the desk, tired of her games. "Well, I did book it, Rosey. A table at an exclusive restaurant that's damn hard to book on short notice. I sent a fucking car to collect you and, guess what, you weren't there."

We sit in silence for a moment and then she sighs, grabbing a burger and beginning to unwrap it. "It'll get cold if we don't eat it now." I shake my head, opening my laptop and ignoring the food. "It's silly to waste it," she adds, and when I still don't grab the burger, she places hers down too. "Albert," she mutters, and I look up, "I don't like fancy restaurants. They don't like me either. It's a mutual thing."

I press my lips together. She's not the sort to apologise, but I think that's the closest I'm gonna get, so I shut the laptop and take a burger. She almost smiles, picking hers up again and taking a bite. When she's like this, she reminds me of a child in trouble. Her small explanations give me insight into the real woman behind this confident mask she puts on for the world.

"Did you sort things with Ollie?"

She nods. "We talked. He's okay. Mav's gonna make him do shit around the clubhouse to keep him busy and away from trouble."

"What about his teacher? Don't you need to meet with her?"

She shrugs. "I'm just gonna let things die down, see how it goes."

"Won't that just make it worse?" I ask, biting into the burger.

"I'm no good with all that stuff," she admits. "Meetings make me nervous."

"You're his mum, don't let them push you around. Tell them you're doing your best and offer to work with them. It'll shut them up. At least that's what my mum used to do."

She smiles. "I can imagine you and Art were a nightmare."

I nod. "Believe it or not, Charlie and Tommy were worse. We were just trying to survive, but that pair," I shake my head, smiling at the memories of my younger siblings, "they were trying to prove something. Ask my mum, she'll tell you horror stories of her school meetings."

"Maybe she can give me some advice," says Rosey, staring down at her burger.

"It must be hard when you're doing it alone," I point out.

She shrugs. "Until recently, I thought I was doing great. When you talk about parenting with any other mother, they'll warn you it's hard when they're small. They'll tell you about sleepless nights and baby blues. But no one talks about the teenage years. Every decision I make might fuck with his head, and my bad choices could lead to him being a shit adult. It's a huge responsibility."

ALBERT

"Maybe don't think of it like that," I tell her. "I mean, I'm no expert, but taking one day at a time seems the obvious choice."

She sighs, placing her half-eaten burger in its wrapper. "Maybe. It's getting late, I should go."

Chapter Four

ROSEY

Albert finishes the last bite of his burger and collects the wrappers. "Thanks," he says, dropping them in the bin. "For feeding me. Although lobster sounded better."

"Your new dancer was good," I say, wandering over to the window and looking out over London. "She's pretty."

"I didn't know you were watching."

"I find it sexy," I admit. "Watching you, watching her." He loosens his tie slightly, and I press my hands against the cool glass of the window. "Did you like watching her?"

I feel him behind me just before his hands wrap around to my front, tugging the button to my jeans. "Not as much as I like watching you," he mutters, pushing my jeans down my legs. He kneels behind me, tapping each ankle, so I lift one at a time until he removes my jeans completely but remains on his knees. His hand runs up my inner thigh until I spread my legs farther apart. It's a dangerous game I'm playing. Each time we do this, I see the need in his eyes. Eventually, he'll want more than what I'm willing to give, and I'll have to let him go. But Albert Taylor isn't like the other men I string along. I don't think he's the type to walk away quietly.

He buries his face between my legs, running his tongue along my opening. His hand joins his tongue, working his fingers into me. It's not long before I'm a quivering mess. He rises to his feet, and I hear his belt being unfastened. The condom wrapper follows, and then he wraps my hair around his fist. Tugging my head back, he pushes his erection at my entrance. "Next time I send a car, you'd better be there," he tells me. "I don't like being stood up." And then he slams into me hard, pushing me against the window.

We dress in silence, awkwardness spreading between us. "I should go," I finally say.

"You said that already," he mutters. "Do you want to tell Archer or should I?" he asks, and I pause, unsure what he means. He sits down behind the desk. "That he's not working for me anymore." He fixes me with a serious look that tells me he's in mobster mode and I should be careful how I answer him.

"What?"

He shrugs. "I told you earlier I'd let him go, and you took a lifeline for him. But you didn't turn up so . . ."

"I had dinner with you," I snap, pointing to the desk. "We just had dinner."

"That wasn't the deal, Red. I booked dinner at a nice restaurant like you requested, and you backed out. Therefore, the deal is off."

"Albert, that's not fair." Archer needs the money, and I desperately want to help him be better. "And besides, he kept his end of the original deal—you're still alive."

He leans forward, resting his elbows on the desk. "Do I look like a man who cares, Red?"

"Be reasonable. Please."

He arches a brow and smirks. "You're begging on his behalf?"

ALBERT

"Look, you're pissed I didn't go on your stupid little date, I get it, but Archer is a nice guy, and he needs the money. I got you dinner, didn't I? We ate together, didn't we?"

"I set the terms, and you didn't pay up. Tell him first thing." I open my mouth to speak, but he gives me that look again. "If you continue to beg for him, I'll think there's more to your working relationship."

I roll my eyes. "I didn't have you down as the jealous type."

He grins. "I'm not. It's about keeping a professional working relationship."

My eyes widen. "Like this?" I snap, pointing between us. "Double standards."

"I'm the boss, I can do what the fuck I like, and right now, I want to get rid of that messy little fucker. So, tell him or don't, either way, he's not on my books anymore." He waits a beat before adding, "Goodbye, Rosey."

As I leave, I'm feeling strange about our encounter. He's never spoken to me like that before. Maybe my instinct was right. Maybe he's getting too attached, which is why he's so pissed about dinner. I groan, knowing I'll have to avoid him, which will be impossible.

I'm not ready to go home. I'm fired up after my fight with Albert, so I head to a wine bar a few streets away from the club.

It's busy as I perch on a seat at the end of the bar and order a cocktail. Damn Meli for abandoning me for Arthur. They want a kid, so he's always dragging her away to the bedroom.

A guy catches my eye. He's holding a bottle just below the bar, and he's emptying a powder into it. He swirls it around and stuffs the packet in his pocket. Then he grabs a second bottle from the bar and looks around. He approaches a woman as she comes from the bathroom. They exchange a few words, and when he offers her the bottle, she smiles politely, shaking her head and moving on. He proceeds to do it a few more times before I catch his eye. It briefly crosses my mind to call for the doormen, but when he pulls up a stool and takes a seat beside me, I decide to hear him out.

"You alone?" he asks. I glance around, pointing out that it's obvious I am. He grins. "Good point. Just thought I'd check."

"Why?"

"Why what?" he asks.

"Why were you checking to see if I'm alone?"

"I can't believe a beautiful woman like you could possibly be here on her own. You must have a husband?"

I scoff. Where do these fuckers come up with this shit? "I'm Rosey," I tell him, holding out a hand. He shakes it, then kisses the back of it, which I immediately wipe away on my jeans.

"Scott."

"Real name or fake?" I ask.

He frowns. "Real."

"Oh. Men like you usually lie."

He pulls out his wallet and produces his driving licence. "See, no lies."

"Are you married?" I ask.

He shakes his head. "No. I like my freedom too much."

"I bet you do," I mutter.

"Drink?" he asks, pointing to the bottle on the bar.

I shake my head. "I don't take drinks from strangers."

He laughs. "What, you think I'd drug it or something?"

"Yes," I say simply, and his smile fades.

"Well, I haven't. See?" He puts the bottle to his lips and tips his head back like he's drank some when it's obvious he hasn't. He slides the bottle to me.

"Look," I say, leaning closer so he catches a glimpse of my chest. "Why don't we cut the small talk? You clearly want a fuck, so just ask me straight."

"Is that what you want?"

I nod, and he grins. "Bring the drink," he says, grabbing my hand and leading me to a back entrance. I grab both bottles, making sure the drugged bottle is closer to him, so I give him that one. We get outside, and I roll my eyes. It's a back alley, so predictable.

"I never met anyone as forward as you," he says, unbuttoning his jeans. I lean back against the wall and hold out the drink. He hesitates, and I smile. "This one was mine," I say, holding it up. "You drank some, right?" He takes his drink and places it on the ground. "Come on, we need to drink if we're gonna get through this," I say, picking it back up and handing it to him. He sighs impatiently, and to placate him, I rub his cock through his jeans. He relaxes, grinning again before downing some of the beer.

ALBERT

He's almost half a bottle down when he frowns and suddenly pulls it away, spitting out a mouthful. "You gave me the wrong bottle," he snaps, wiping his tongue like that'll work.

I laugh. "I don't know what you mean. Didn't we have the same?"

"Let's just get on with this," he snaps, shoving his jeans down and fisting his erection.

I raise my brows. "There's not much there," I say, tipping my head to one side and eyeing his small cock. "I mean, I could maybe do something with it but..." I shake my head, "Actually, I can't. It's way too small."

"What the fuck are you talking about?"

"Your cock," I say, nodding at it. "It's not big enough."

He narrows his eyes, rage filling him. "Get on your fucking knees, bitch, and I'll show you how big it is when you're choking on it."

I throw my head back laughing. "Does that work on others? Do they actually get on their knees and pretend to enjoy your tiny penis?"

"Bitch, I swear, you'll fucking—"

"Pay?" I finish for him, grinning. "You're probably right, it would feel like a payment if I was to put that anywhere near my mouth. Nope, I mean charity, not payment." I fold my arms. "Now, let's rewind to the start. When you got the bottles of beer, you fucked up. No woman will willingly take a drink you bought in advance. It screams date rape. And for the record, you weren't very discreet back there. I saw the whole thing."

He puts his cock away, fastening his trousers. "Fuck you," he spits and then suddenly grabs onto the wall for support.

"Are you alright there? You look a little drowsy." I smirk as he leans against the bricks and closes his eyes. "And when you gave me your real name, that kind of made it weird. You either don't give a shit if you get caught or you were planning on making sure I couldn't tell anyone. Were you going to kill me, Scott?"

He mumbles something, shaking his head. I take his beer bottle and hold it to his lips. He tries to shake me off, but he slides down the wall instead, losing his balance. I grip his face and tip his head back, pouring the liquid down his throat. He chokes, spitting some out but swallowing the rest. I unfasten his jeans, retrieving his flaccid cock and taking out my pocketknife. "Now, I'm letting you off lightly because not only are you getting to walk away from this, but you'll also not remember the pain. Thank the lord for date rape drugs, yay," I say, smirking as I hack away at his lump of flesh.

"Do I wanna know?" comes Albert's voice, and I smile to myself. He's keeping tabs on me.

I turn to him, holding up the severed penis. "Did you know, some people keep this sort of thing as a trophy?"

He screws up his face in disgust. "I doubt many people go around cutting off men's penises," he says dryly.

"He doesn't deserve one. He was using it for bad things." I drop it in a nearby storm drain, smiling when I hear the plop as it hits the water.

"Mav called. He couldn't get hold of you. Someone is at the clubhouse looking for you."

"At one in the morning? Did he say who?"

Albert shakes his head and moves closer to the guy. "Is he dead?"

"No. He should live, so he can think about why this happened to him." Albert hands me a handkerchief, and I take it gratefully to wipe my hands.

I offer it back, and he shakes his head. "Keep it."

ALBERT

I drive Rosey back to the clubhouse. She doesn't ask me to, we just leave the alleyway together and she gets into the car with me. I spoke with the doormen, and they're gonna wipe any CCTV for the evening, but as a precaution, I've arranged for Rosey's penis-less man to be dumped outside the hospital.

I follow her towards the door of the clubhouse, and she turns to face me. "How did you know where I was?"

I smirk. "I followed my nose." I open the door and head inside without telling her the truth, that her phone is now also tracked, thanks to my brother.

Mav's sitting with a woman I don't recognise. Rosey steps in behind me, and they both stand, Mav looking slightly apprehensive. I turn to Rosey to find her rooted to the spot. She looks shocked, and for a second, I consider standing between her and this stranger until I know she's happy to speak with her.

"Mum?" she murmurs, and my eyes widen. As far as I knew, her mother's not been on the scene for a long time.

"Rosey," says the woman, smiling. "It's great to see you."

"What are you doing here?" she asks.

Her mum huffs with a laugh. "That's all you have to say?"

ALBERT

"It's after one in the morning, and it's been years since we spoke. The last I heard, you were in Ireland."

"Should we all sit down and discuss things?" asks Mav.

Rosey shakes her head. "No. No, we shouldn't. I can't do this right now." And she heads back out.

Mav goes to follow, but I hold up a hand. "I'll go. If that's okay?" He nods, and I rush after her. She's waiting by my car, and I smile to myself, clicking the button to unlock it. She gets in, slamming the door and staring straight ahead.

I slide into the driver's side and start the engine. "Are you—"

"I don't want to talk about it."

I nod. "Noted."

She remains silent until I stop outside my house. I've never brought anyone back here . . . well, not a woman at least. I get out and round the vehicle, opening her door. She looks lost in thought until I hold out my hand, which seems to break her daydream. She offers a weak smile and takes it, and I lead her towards the house. She follows me inside. "Nice place," she comments, shrugging from her jacket.

"Drink?" I ask, leading her to the kitchen.

She shakes her head. "I think I've had enough."

"You want me to call Mav and see if she's gone?" She shakes her head again. "Well, I've got a couple spare rooms, so take your pick."

I show her upstairs to the spare room closest my own. Before I leave, she places a kiss on my cheek. "Thanks for bringing me back here, letting me crash. I appreciate it." I nod, then leave her to rest.

I don't sleep well, I never do, but tonight is especially hard knowing Rosey is right next door to me. I've almost bust in there more times than I care to think about, but I've managed to keep control of myself.

By seven a.m., I give up and head downstairs. It's minutes later when Rosey comes down fully dressed. "You're up early," I say. "Coffee?"

She looks uncomfortable. "No, I should go. Ollie needs to be up for school."

"I'll take you back," I offer, grabbing my car keys.

"It's not a good idea," she says, "but thanks."

I scoff. "It's just a lift home, Red, not a marriage proposal."

She rests her hands on the worktop. "Don't you think we're getting too comfortable?"

"No."

"Because we're doing married couple shit. Before you know it, we'll be talking to one another in the bathroom while one of us is on the toilet."

I laugh. "You're overthinking."

She nods. "I know, I do it a lot, but it's making me crazy, so we should just . . . yah know, not do this." She swirls her hands between us, and I frown. "I'll see you around."

"Most likely, seeing as you work for me," I say, smirking.

"I don't . . . technically, I'm self-employed. And I'm semi-retired. Archer works for you now . . . right?"

"So, that's what this is about? We talked already, Red—" I begin, but she cuts me off.

"I know but hear me out. I'll spend some real time with him, make sure he's clear on the rules. If he fucks up again, I'll fully back you. And I'm saving you having to find someone else."

"I wouldn't have to. I have you."

"Semi-retired still," she says, shrugging. "See yah." And then she bounces out the door like an energised puppy dog, and my head is reeling.

Chapter Five

ROSEY

Mav's waiting when I return. I try to pass his office, but he steps in my path, halting me. "Office, now," he orders. I groan like a stroppy teenager and head in behind him. "You ran out," he says. "What the fuck, Rosey?"

"I didn't wanna see her," I tell him, shrugging.

"Still the same fucking Rosey," he mutters, shaking his head. "Running at the first sign of difficulty."

"Difficulty doesn't bother me, Mav. I kill for a living," I remind him.

"But anything emotional and off you run."

"I haven't seen her in years, and she's not seen Ollie since he was small. I have nothing to say to her."

"But she clearly has shit to say to you, and if I know Connie, she'll just keep coming back until she's said what she came to say."

I chew on my lower lip, thinking over his words. "What did she say?" I reluctantly ask.

"She's been back in London for six months."

I roll my eyes. "Yet this is the first time she's come to see me?"

"Apparently, she didn't know where you were. She tried your old haunts and came here just in case."

"You shouldn't have told her I was back here," I mutter. "Then she'd have left."

"I thought it might help you to have her back in your life," he begins, perching on the edge of his desk. "I know you're struggling with Ollie, so maybe having your mum around might help?"

"I don't see how, Mav. She was hardly mother of the year."

He nods in understanding. "I know, but she looks clean, Rosey. I wouldn't have told her you were here if I thought she was still using." He hands me a piece of paper. "She left her address. Go and see her, find out what she wants. It could be what you and Ollie need right now."

Archer yawns. "Were you up all night studying the human body?" I ask, arching a brow.

He smirks. "Not exactly. I mean, I was examining a human body, but not in the way you want me to."

"Albert is keen on getting rid of you," I confess, and he sits up straighter. "He hates the mess. I told you it would come back to bite you."

"I made a deal," he snaps. "He gets to live, and I get regular work."

"Relax," I mutter. "I smoothed it over with him for now, but you gotta take it seriously, Archer. The Taylors never let outsiders in, and they took a chance with you. If you carry on ignoring my advice, who knows how it'll end."

"Are you saying they'd take me out?"

"I'm saying keep your head down and take fucking notes on how to kill without leading the police to your damn door." I stop the car outside Ollie's school and take a calming breath. "Right, I should go in," I mutter. "Don't do anything stupid while I'm gone."

"I'll come in. I'm good with this sort of thing," he says, following me out the car.

"How come? You got a secret kid I know nothing about?"

He laughs. "Fuck no. I have younger brothers."

We head into the reception area, where I'm greeted by a stony-faced woman. "I'm here to see the head teacher for Ollie," I tell her. She slides a book to me and hands me a pen. "Sign in?" I ask, because she's clearly forgot how to speak. I scribble my name, and Archer does the same.

Mrs. Ball steps from her office, forcing a smile as she takes in Archer. "I'm Ollie's head teacher, Mrs. Ball," she says, holding out her hand. Archer shakes it but offers no explanation. "And you are?" she pushes.

"Archer," he says.

She glances at me for more, but I smile awkwardly and offer nothing. "Are you a relation to Ollie?" she asks, leading us into her office.

"Yep," he says, sitting down. I sit beside him.

"Right. Well, we should start with Ollie's lesson attendance."

"I've been dropping him at the door every day," I tell her. "I can't walk him to each lesson."

ALBERT

"Even when he decides to attend lessons, he often walks out before the end."

"I asked him about it. I even had his half-brother speak to him," I say. "He promised he'd make an effort." She makes a note on some paper. "Does he have friends?" I ask. Ollie doesn't mention anyone apart from Ben, who I've never met, and he never brings anyone home.

"You tell me," she says.

I hesitate. "He doesn't talk about friends."

"The group he's in with aren't exactly a good influence. All of them are older," she tells me. "Does he go out after school?"

I nod. "Most nights."

"And I take it you know where he is?"

I shrug. "He's twelve. Who knows where their twelve-year-old is at every minute of every day."

She narrows her eyes. "Most people do, actually."

Archer sits up straighter. "What's the point of this meeting?" he asks.

"I'd like to work with you on how we approach Ollie to get him to participate in his learning."

"But his learning is down to you. Keeping him in lessons is down to you. Rosey's job is to parent, yours is to teach.

If you don't know how to handle a difficult child, that's a 'you' problem."

Her face reddens slightly, and I worry she's about to burst, so I gently pat Archer's arm to shut him up. "I'll speak to him again. I'll get him to school every day on time. His older brother is getting him work outside of school to keep him occupied. I'm trying my best, Mrs. Ball. And if he walks out on a lesson, call me, and I'll come and drag him back."

She nods stiffly. "It's a plan, I suppose."

"He's surrounded by family, they all care for him, and I'll make sure he knows we're supporting him, as are you. Just stick with us while we work on him."

As we head back to the car, I check my phone to find several missed calls from Albert. I groan. The last thing I need is him on my back, but it's best to face him head-on, so I drive right to the office.

"Don't piss him off," I warn Archer as we head inside.

He grins innocently. "As if I would."

I knock on the office door, and it's Arthur who tells us to enter. I glance at Archer. "I swear, don't get us killed today," I hiss as we enter.

"Finally," snaps Arthur.

ALBERT

"Sorry, I was in a meeting," I offer feebly.

"And it was so important you couldn't answer the damn phone?"

"It was on silent," I mutter.

Arthur rubs his chin thoughtfully. "I'm starting to feel nervous," he says. "I need people around me who have their eye on the ball."

"I do," I say.

He arches a brow at my blatant disrespect. "You've lost that sassy attitude, Red. Without it, you're not as appealing."

"What are you saying? You don't wanna use my services?"

"I'm saying get your shit together," he says firmly, staring me down.

I nod. "Noted."

"Sit," says Albert, and I do. "I need you on the streets watching out for these," he tells me, placing some photographs on the table. I glance at the surveillance pictures of a group of youths. "They're trying to move in on our patch."

I scowl. "That's not my line of work. Ask Ghost."

He slams his hand on the table, and I jump. "Your line of work is whatever we tell you it is." I eye him angrily. The sudden change in his attitude towards me is pissing me off.

I take a calming breath and arch my brow. "I think you'll find my work is tailored to specific skills."

"Are you telling me you don't watch your victims before you land a kill?" he asks.

"I'm telling you I don't follow kids around because they're selling drugs on your streets." I stand. "Feel free to put a bullet in me if you're done with me. You'll do us all a favour." I leave the office, slamming the door behind me.

ALBERT

Archer presses his lips together and taps his fingers on the arm of the chair. "Should I just . . ." He nods at the door.

"What meeting was she at?" I ask.

"Her son's school."

"And she took you along?"

He nods. "She needed back-up. That teacher was a dragon." He rises to his feet and heads for the door. "Yah know, she's struggling right now. It might be helpful to know that before you yell at her. You know what she's like when she gets pissed at the world, we're all in danger." He grins and leaves.

I turn to my brother and sigh heavily. "We never should have started using her, Art. She's a fucking liability."

He smirks. "In or out the bedroom?"

"She doesn't do anything she's told to do."

"That's what I like about her, Bert. It gets boring being surrounded by yes men. Anyway, why do you want her watching the streets? We didn't discuss that."

"I got a feeling her kid's in trouble. He was on their turf a few days back. Rosey had to pick him up when his mates did a runner, leaving him alone. He looked scared, and he knew that wasn't our territory yet."

"Have you taken it to Mav?"

I shake my head. "She asked me not to. She seems to think the kid's just having a bad time. She thinks she's got it in hand."

"And you don't agree?"

I shake my head. "He's running with gangs. He's out of his depth."

"And you could see all that from one fuck-up? Maybe he just wandered onto the wrong side by mistake."

"You didn't see him. He was skittish, like he knew he was in danger. How would he know that if he was an innocent kid?"

Arthur shrugs. "Put Wild Coyote on it. Maybe if he's watching them, he'll be less likely to paint the town red with blood."

Alex sways to the hypnotic sound of the music. The smirk on her red painted lips makes me want to put her over my knee. She drops to her knees and crawls across the floor towards me, stopping by my feet and running her red nails over my thighs. The door swings open and Rosey strolls in like she isn't interrupting my private dance. I groan in frustration.

"This is a private room," I remind her as Alex continues stroking my thigh. "Ignore her," I snap. "Continue." She nods, staying on her knees as she slowly removes her bra.

Rosey drops down on the plush seat beside me. "We need to talk."

"I've been in my office all fucking day. Can't you stick to normal hours?"

ALBERT

"My job isn't the usual nine-to-five," she points out.

Alex slides up my body, making sure to press her breasts against me. "And whatever you need to chat about couldn't wait?"

"Not really."

Alex sits over me, her mouth inches from my own. "Spit it out, so I can get on with my night," I snap. I've been trying to hold Rosey at arm's length because the second she thinks I'm getting too close, she backs off, and frankly, I'm bored of chasing her.

Alex rocks against me, and I feel my cock begin to stir to life. She holds onto my shoulders, gently digging her nails into the skin. "Archer said you've put him on kid watch," says Rosey.

"So?"

"Why?"

Alex nibbles my ear, and I glance at Rosey, who's watching the interaction. "What the fuck's it got to do with you?"

"I thought I was training him."

I grip Alex's hair, twisting it around my fist and pulling her mouth to mine. She runs her tongue over my lower lip, and I grin. "Go home, Rosey. Spend time with your kid like you wanted."

"That sounds like employee discrimination," she snaps.

"Didn't you tell me you weren't my employee? Anyway, fucking sue me. Now, get out. I need some time away from you and Archer and anything business-related."

I feel her eyes on me as I consume Alex's mouth. I pull her against me, enjoying the feel of her. She fumbles with my belt, and I hear Rosey mutter something about breaking the rules of the club. She's right, there's a no-touching rule, but that doesn't apply when you're the boss. I hear the door close and relax, letting Alex slide back down my body as she releases my zipper.

Chapter Six

ROSEY

I stand outside Albert's private room, feeling enraged. He kicked me out so he could fuck the dancer. I should be happy, as he's clearly not as hung up on me as I thought, but I don't feel happy at all. In fact, there's a definite pain where my heart should be, and that's a rarity for me.

I scowl, heading back out to the bar. Fuck him. I don't need Albert Taylor. As I walk through, I turn heads, and it's the boost I need. I grab the tie of a good-looking man and bring him close, pressing my mouth against his. He wastes no time in grabbing a handful of my arse, and I let him because I need to feel something instead of the usual numbness. When he pushes me against the wall, I shudder.

I can't do this, not with some random guy. I push him away. "Hey," he complains.

"I changed my mind," I mutter, taking his drink from his hand and knocking it back. "Now, fuck off."

I turn back towards the room I just vacated, wild thoughts racing through my mind. Before I can overthink it, I march back inside with purpose. Albert growls, "What now?" before spotting me. His expression changes and his eyes become hooded. Alex is back on her feet, dancing sexily. I straddle Albert, grabbing his face in my hands and kissing him hard. He lets me, while running his hands up my thighs. I release his erection, taking it in both hands and rubbing slowly. He hisses, his head falling back.

"Watch her," I whisper, nipping the skin below his ear. His eyes open, fixed on her, as I work him, rubbing his cock while kissing him hungrily. He suddenly holds my wrists, keeping me still.

"Alex, leave," he barks, and I smirk. The second she leaves, he stands, wrapping my legs around his waist and backing me against the wall. "For a second there, I thought you were giving up," he murmurs, kissing me.

"I don't want a relationship," I whisper, pulling my skirt to my waist.

He grins against my mouth. "Good. I don't do relationships." He moves my knickers to one side and eases into me. "But when you're fucking me, it's only gonna be me. Understand?"

"Too exclusive," I mutter, closing my eyes and enjoying the feel of him filling me up. "Fuck who you want."

He grazes my shoulder with his teeth. "Don't test me, Red. I don't share."

"Take me as I am." He withdraws and slams into me hard, causing my body to jolt. "Fuck," I cry.

"I'll kill every man you fuck that isn't me," he warns, then he places his hand over my mouth to stop me answering. He fucks me hard until I orgasm, pulling out right before he comes and pushing me to my knees. I take him in my mouth and swallow his release.

I stand, straightening my clothes as he tucks himself away. "Business and pleasure remain separate," he says, "but I meant what I said."

"Albert—" I begin, but he cuts me off with a glare.

"I'll take you home."

ALBERT

Rosey was jealous. That's the reason she came back into that room. She might not be ready to admit it, but I know I'm right, and even though we're not ready for anything serious, I'm pushing her for exclusive sex. What's the point in denying what we clearly both need from each other?

We get in the car, and she hands me a piece of paper. "I need to go here."

I frown. "It's almost midnight."

"I can read the time, Albert. Are you going to take me, or should I call a cab?"

I drive, heading for the address. "It's right on the boarder to the Abbey Estate," I say. "Is there a reason you want to head into a territory we're fighting to own?" She remains silent, and it annoys me. "Red, if you're going to see a guy—"

"What if I am, Albert?" she snaps, turning to face me. "What if I'm about to go fuck another man and—"

I pull the car onto the road's edge and slam on the brakes. I grip the steering wheel tightly. "You can keep fighting me on this," I warn, "or you could just accept we're happening and there ain't shit you can do about it."

She stares forward, her arms folded stubbornly across her chest. "Why me?"

ALBERT

"What do you mean?"

"Why are you so obsessed with having me to yourself?"

I turn to her, grabbing her chin in my fingers and forcing her to look me in the eye. "I already have you, Red. You're mine, you just don't want to conform. But you will, trust me on that. Now, tell me where the fuck we're going."

She hesitates before saying, "To see my mum."

I release her and put the car back into drive. "See, that was easy."

We arrive outside a block of flats. There are groups of youths hanging around despite the time. It's something we need to get a handle on, so we can win the trust of the residents here. I get out of the car, and Rosey eyes me. "I don't need you to come in."

"I wasn't waiting for permission," I counter.

She rolls her eyes and leads the way. We pass a large group of youths who nod in greeting, and I fix the biggest of the group with a glare. "Anything happens to that car," I say, pointing to where my car is parked, "I'll come for you."

He nods. "Got it, Mr. Taylor." And then, he rides his bike towards it.

We climb three flights of stairs because the elevators are out of action. Rosey checks the address on the piece of paper again before knocking on the door. A man yells something inaudible before her mum pulls the door open, her expression one of anger. It soon dissolves when she sees her daughter. "Rosey," she whispers, glancing behind her nervously before stepping out into the passageway and pulling the door to, "I didn't expect you."

"Why give me your address if you don't want me to show up?" she asks.

"That's not what I meant. I just didn't think you'd come here. Have you seen the time?"

Rosey glances at her watch. "I find the best time to catch someone off guard is during the night."

"What did you expect to find me doing?" her mum asks with a nervous laugh.

"The usual," says Rosey. "Selling yourself, getting high."

Her mum looks guilty. "That's not me anymore, Rosey. I'm a different person. It's why I reached out—"

"Who the fuck are you talking to?" a man yells from inside.

"Rosey," she shouts back. "She's with Mr. Taylor." He doesn't bother to reply, and Rosey's mum smiles awkwardly. "Maybe we can meet for coffee one day . . . away from here?"

"Don't you want to introduce me to whoever you have in there?" asks Rosey.

"Not really. He's not good with visitors, especially people he doesn't know. He's not always here. He'll be gone most of tomorrow if you want to come back."

Rosey shrugs. "I'll think about it." And then she walks away, and I follow.

As we descend the steps, I take her hand. She scowls, pulling it free again, and I smirk. "You okay?"

"Why wouldn't I be?" she snaps.

"Are you coming back tomorrow?"

"I haven't decided."

"I think you want to," I say.

"You don't know me," she mutters. "Don't pretend you do."

ROSEY

He unnerves me. I've never let any man take control the way I let him, and it's messing with my head. The way he demands my time turns me on. Usually, I'd punch a man in the face if he spoke to me the way he does, but he's not taking my shit and I kind of like it.

We get in the car, and he starts the engine. "Where to?" he asks.

"Home," I mutter, staring out the window. Something felt off about Mum. She was nervous, and she was definitely hiding whoever she had in her flat. It wouldn't be the first time she's gotten into a relationship with a guy who's been a complete dick. She's the reason I've never settled down . . . just in case I've inherited her bad taste. I glance over at Arthur. His brow is furrowed as he slips in and out of the night traffic. I place my hand on his thigh and slide it up towards his crotch. He gives a side glance, a smirk pulling on his lips.

"You can't use sex to hide your feelings," he says.

I feel his cock stiffen. "Stop talking," I mutter, unfastening my seat belt and reaching over to open his trousers. I take out his erection, and he hisses.

"Red, it's dangerous," he murmurs, watching as I lower my mouth to him.

"I love danger," I whisper, taking his cock in my mouth.

"Fuck," he moans. I feel the car begin to slow, then he turns off the engine. "Home," he mutters, unfastening his own seat belt and pushing his chair farther back.

I release him from my mouth and grab onto his shoulders, lifting myself to sit over him. I move my knickers to one side and slide down his length, loving the feel of him inside me. I ride him fast, rushing to get my orgasm. He lets me, and after I come, he lifts me and fists his cock, pumping it a few more times until he comes. I watch it run over his hand and smile. "Thanks for the ride," I say, smirking, then I open his car door and get out, pulling my skirt into place.

"You're not inviting me in?" he asks, arching a brow.

I shake my head. "Not tonight, Bert." I close the door and head into the clubhouse.

At breakfast the next morning, Meli sits beside me. "Why do you always come here for breakfast?" asks Mav. "Don't you have food in your place?"

"I like to annoy you," she retorts, grabbing a pancake and placing it on her plate. "I feel like we never spend time together anymore," she complains to me.

I sigh. "I went to the club with you, and you left me for Arthur," I remind her.

She grins. "He's persuasive."

"You've become one of those girls who gets a boyfriend and dumps her friends."

She wiggles her wedding ring in my face. "I'm a married woman, I have to put his needs first. Who are you sleeping with lately? You never tell me anything."

I laugh. "You never ask."

"I'm asking now. I feel I'm missing out on single life, so I'm living it through you. Tell me it's Archer," she says wistfully.

"He's pretty to look at," I admit. Albert clears his throat from behind me, and I jump in fright. *When the hell did he get here?*

"Don't let me stop you," he says, sitting the other side of me as Mama B hands him a coffee.

"Why are you here?" I ask.

"I've got a meeting with Mav," he says, stirring his coffee. "Continue, I want to hear all about you and Archer."

ALBERT

"So, you are sleeping with him?" Meli gasps.

I feel uncomfortable. "No, of course not."

"But you want to," she says excitedly.

"It sounds like you want to," Albert confirms.

"Christ, I just want to eat my breakfast," I snap. Ollie saunters in half-dressed for school. "I'll drive you," I tell him. "Eat something, you have five minutes."

"I'm walking," he mutters, not bothering to look at me.

"I promised I'd get you to school," I say, standing.

"I can get myself to school," he snaps angrily, and Mav and Albert stand at the same time.

"Watch your fucking mouth," Mav growls.

"I'll take you to school," adds Albert. "Get your shit together now."

The kitchen clears soon after, leaving me alone with Mama B, who takes the opportunity to join me at the table. "You okay?"

I nod. "Why does everyone keep asking me that?"

She shrugs. "You look different, Rosey. Not your usual self."

"I'm fine."

"You can talk to me," she offers.

"Isn't that weird for you?" I ask, curiosity getting the better of me.

She shakes her head and smiles kindly. "Why would it be? You're a member of this club just like any other."

"I went to see my mum last night," I blurt out, unable to stop it.

She looks surprised. "How did it go?"

"I don't understand why she's back." I scrub my face with my hands. "Everything seems to be spiralling at the moment. Mum being back, Ollie acting . . . well, acting like a teenager. I just feel like I'm losing grip on life."

"Teenagers are hard work," she admits. "Maverick was so much harder than the girls."

"Really?" I ask with a laugh. "Even harder than Meli?"

She laughs too. "Meli was hard, but Mav was a testosterone-filled boy with anger problems. He looked up to his father so much, and when he began to see him for what he was, he didn't know how to deal with that."

"I remember his outbursts," I say.

"He wouldn't listen to me because he thought I was weak. Eagle pushed me around, and I guess I looked weak, but it took strength to survive him for my kids. And survive him, I did." She takes my hand, something she's never done, and emotions swirl around inside. "It's hard work when you have to be strong all the time. Even harder work when you're acting."

"How did you get through to Mav in the end?" I ask.

She grins. "A few slaps, a lot of threats, and taking a step back."

"Really?"

"Sometimes, they need to make their own mistakes to see the truth. Ollie's a boy in a man's world, and he's trying to find his place. But you need to remind him he's here because you raised him. There was a time in his life when all he had was you. Take control and show him he can't treat you like shit."

"Did it help?" I ask. "Having Eagle around?"

She scoffs. "That man almost ruined my life and my kids. If I could turn back time, I'd have left long ago and taken my babies with me. Mav saw way too much for his young age, and the girls . . . well, the emotional damage is one thing, but he sat back and allowed Meli to be hurt physically. If I could go back, I'd have killed the motherfucker a long time ago."

"I guess Ollie's lucky he never got to know him."

"Very lucky. Now, chin up, cos we miss that sassy mouth of yours."

Chapter Seven

ALBERT

Mav looks over the map and nods in agreement. "All of this area is open for us to take," I say. "If we move now, we'll get control easily."

"And you don't think it's too much when we're fighting for the Abbey Road estate?"

"No. We're already out there making noise, we may as well take it all."

"Okay. I'll take it to church and vote on it, but I think we'll be good to go. I can have men out there tonight cleaning up the gangs if you get the word out."

I nod, folding the map. "I'll let Art know you're in. We can move right away. I have men visiting bar owners as we speak. We're offering the usual rate for protection with a discount for anyone who gives up info."

We shake on it, and I head out, but instead of leaving, I go up to Rosey's room. If she's going to get the message that she's mine, I need to be present. I find her laying on her bed, staring at her iPad. She glances up. "I'm busy."

"I'm not in the mood for your mouth today," I tell her, fisting her hair and turning her away from me. I use my free hand to grab her leggings and tug them down far enough to expose her. "Talking about that messy son of a bitch with Meli like a fan girl," I add, releasing myself. "He's a fucking boy, Red. Is that what you want?" She tries to nod, and I slap her thigh. "Bullshit. He couldn't handle you." I ease into her, and she groans. "You need a man to take the amount of shit you throw." I fuck her hard until she comes and then pull out, spilling myself onto her backside. "You need to be on the pill," I mutter, rubbing my sticky mess into her skin.

"Who says I'm not?" she asks, arching a brow as I tuck myself away. I pull her leggings back into place. "I checked your medical record," I admit, and she narrows her eyes. "You're an employee, I get to see that shit."

"I didn't give you permission."

ALBERT

I lean down, kissing her on the forehead, and she scowls. "I'll pick you up later."

"What for?"

I shrug. "I haven't decided yet."

ROSEY

He leaves, and I smile to myself. He keeps on coming back, even when I tell him not to. I like it.

I meet Archer after lunch so we can go over our plan. I've been hired to take out a Paedophile. It's not uncommon, especially in this case, where the customer went through the proper channels, but the court system failed her. She's been biding her time for three years for this moment.

"Wait in the bathroom until I get him up to the room. Don't come out until I say the keyword." I don't usually share my work like this, but he needs to practise a clean kill away from Albert's eyes.

"And what's the word again?" he asks.

I roll my eyes. "Scumbag," I tell him for the fifth time as I hand him the key card for the room. It's a shady hotel that's used by prostitutes and drug dealers mainly, but it's perfect for jobs like this. I hired the room for two days, so his body won't be found straight away, and when I check out, it's not a face-to-face deal. I can just leave the key card in the bin on the reception desk. "And don't forget to cover your face as we go in. It's the only camera in the place," I remind him. The chances are it doesn't work. These places tend to forget to fix cameras or the police would forever be in here taking footage to catch wanted criminals.

We head inside separately. I go for the bar, where I've already arranged to meet Tim Holden. He's bigger than I imagined. The pictures I saw in his file showed him looking thinner and weaker. He's clearly been working out since then. I sit beside him, and he side eyes me. "Katy?" he murmurs, and I nod. "You alone?"

I glance around like I'm nervous. "My friend is picking her up from nursery as we speak. She'll meet us up there."

"One hour, like we agreed?" he asks, and I nod. He slides an envelope towards me, and I take it, tucking it inside my jacket. "Whatever I like, right?" I nod again, sickness swirling inside my stomach. "How many times you done this?"

"What's it matter?" I snap impatiently. "Are you a cop or something?" I stand, and he looks panic stricken.

"No, no, of course not. I just didn't know how far I could take it is all. Like, is she experienced?"

ALBERT

I sit back down. "She's four years old," I hiss. "Just do what you gotta do." I pretend to check my mobile then nod. "She's almost here. We should go up to the room and wait."

He follows me, and I make sure to hide my face as we head for the elevator. I pull out the spare key card and head to the room, stepping inside. "How many times have you done this?" I ask, clicking the lock on the door.

He takes a seat on the bed, shrugging from his jacket. "It's surprising how many so-called mothers will sell their daughters for money," he mutters.

"That would surprise me," I reply, and he catches my eye, sensing the change. "You ever do it without the mother's knowledge?"

He frowns. "What do you mean?"

"Yah know, girlfriend's kids." I shrug. "That must be easier than paying?"

"A few times," he admits, "but I get bored easily. Eventually, they stop fighting me and it loses the thrill."

I turn my back to him, wincing at his words. *Piece of shit*. "Do you ever think it's wrong?" I ask, turning back to face him.

He shrugs. "No. Love comes in all kinds of forms."

I arch a brow. "You think it's love?"

"Don't judge me," he snaps. "You're the one here selling your kid."

"Oh, about that," I begin. "I don't have a daughter."

"Huh?"

"I don't have a daughter. I lied."

He rises to his feet, and I'm again aware of his size. "What the fuck are you talking about?"

"I have a son. He's out of your age range, although I know you're not fussy on the sex. But trust me when I say, you wouldn't want my kid, he's a prick at the minute. I guess teenagers are, though, right?"

"What the hell is going on?"

"He's going off the rails, and I have no idea how to stop him. Is that what happened to you?" I ask, tipping my head to the side. "Did you go off the rails and stick your dick in a child?"

"Bitch, you've made a mistake," he murmurs.

"I don't think so. You're a scumbag, I'm a killer—we're the perfect pair." I wait for Archer to appear at my use of the code word, but he doesn't. I glance at the bathroom door. "I said, scumbag," I repeat. He still doesn't appear, and I turn back to Tim and eye up his size again. "Fuck," I mutter.

"What's your plan?" he asks, grinning.

"I was hoping I could sit back and watch your demise, but it seems my partner in crime is MIA." I sigh heavily. "And I'll be honest, Tim, I wasn't planning on getting dirty today. I'm wearing white," I point out, glancing at my shirt. "Blood is the worst kind of stain to get out of whites." I shrug. "This is why I like to work alone. You can never rely on anyone."

"You think you can take me down?" he asks, smirking. "Come on then, little lady, take your shot. I'll give you a free one." He holds his hands out. I know to take this guy out, I need to be closer, but the second I move to him, he's going to punch me. And with a guy of his size, he'll likely knock me out.

"Maybe I got this wrong," I begin, backing to the door. "Maybe we should forget this." I turn my back to him and fiddle with the lock. It works and he comes at me, pressing me against the door.

"I came for a fuck," he hisses in my ear. "I ain't leaving until I get one."

"Aren't I a little old for you?" I muse. He presses his erection to my arse, and I roll my eyes.

"A cunt is a cunt," he growls.

I shove back off the door, and he stumbles slightly. I dive at him, shoving him back onto the bed. "I hate that word," I snap. "There are so many more words out there equally as offensive but less disgusting," I tell him.

He doesn't gauge the danger he's in. Instead, his hands glide up my ribs to my breasts. "I love a fight," he murmurs, groping me.

He uses his weight to spin us so I'm beneath him and takes full advantage of his freedom to place his hands where he likes. I fidget, and he presses his erection against my core. It's the distraction he needs while I twist to retrieve the knife from my ankle. At that moment, the door busts open and Tim is ripped from me. I push onto my elbows to find Albert holding him against the wall with a gun to his head. "What the fuck?" I snap.

"Did he touch you?" he demands to know.

"Bert, I'm at work," I say, exasperated.

A small pop sounds out and the guy slumps. Albert drops him to the ground and turns back to me. "He had his fucking hands on what's mine," he growls.

ALBERT

Archer appears in the doorway. "Sorry, the key card wouldn't..." He trails off, taking in the scene before him. "Fuck, I missed it?"

I flop back onto the bed and groan loudly. "What the fuck has my life become?"

"You mean you were meant to be here?" asks Albert.

"I couldn't get in, and by the time I found a staff member to sort it—"

I pinch the bridge of my nose. "You spoke to a staff member?" Albert repeats.

"Well, yeah, I needed to sort the card."

Albert glares at me. "Do you see what I mean?" he snaps. "A liability!"

I sit up. "Why are you here, Albert?"

"You were in a hotel, what the fuck was I meant to think?"

I glare at him angrily. "You're tracking me?"

He hesitates. It's the first time he's said it out loud. "Well, yeah. We track all our employees."

"Including Archer?" I ask, arching my brow, and he nods. "So, you thought I was in here with him?"

"It's a good job I came in when I did because that guy was on top of you, Red!"

I throw my knife and it slices into the wooden door, missing Albert by inches. His eyes widen. "Seriously!" he yells.

"I had it under control," I say through gritted teeth.

ALBERT

She stands, retrieving her knife from the door. "Clean this mess up yourself, I'm done," she growls, storming out.

Archer shifts uncomfortably. "You want me to sort it?"

I almost laugh. "No, Archer. No, I don't. Go get any CCTV from today and pray to fucking God the employee doesn't recognise you if the police chase this clusterfuck."

"She won't. She was more than accommodating."

I glare at his smirk. "What?"

"Yah know, she was happy to help," he says, winking.

I grab his collar and shove him against the wall. "You were fucking some bitch instead of watching Rosey?"

"Rosey can handle herself," he argues.

"Get the hell out of my sight right now before I put you in the ground."

ALBERT

Rosey ignores my calls, and when I go to the clubhouse, she's not there. But I find her at Bertie's propping up the bar and chatting with my bar staff. When she sees me, she turns her back, clearly ignoring me.

"This is bullshit," I whisper into her ear from behind her. "You're mad I saved you?"

She spins to face me, her expression angry. "I don't need saving, Albert. I do just fine on my own."

She's drunk. "Doesn't it get tiring?" I ask, stroking a finger down her cheek. "Pretending you've got your shit together?" I walk away and head to the office, giving her the time she needs to calm down.

It's almost an hour later when security calls me and asks me to come and get her from the bar. I head right down to where she's arguing with my bar staff for another drink. We have a policy that we don't serve to anyone who appears drunk. She doesn't see me coming, so I grip her upper arm, pulling her away from the bar and back towards my office.

Once we're inside, she pulls free, turning on me. "How dare you?" she screams. I sit behind my desk and go back to the email I was reading. "And for the record, I'm not pretending. I never said I had my shit together." I continue to ignore her. "And I don't need you turning up when I'm on a job to rescue me. I can take down any fucking man, including Tim fucking Holden."

I lean back and sigh. "Finished?" She folds her arms over her chest. "Good. Sit the fuck down and drink some water." I nod at the leather couch. She snatches a whiskey bottle from the liquor cabinet and takes a seat. I decide not to rise to it, picking my battles wisely.

Chapter Eight

ROSEY

Why do I follow his orders? The question plays over in my mind while I drink from his expensive whiskey bottle. He just has this way that makes me stop and listen. No one's done that to me since . . . I shudder with repulsion. *Since Eagle*. I shake my head to clear his image from my mind. Eagle was different. I was just a kid, and he scared the shit out of me. I've grown up since then.

I watch Albert type away on his laptop, paying me no attention. I hate that he's ignoring me. I swig some more from the bottle and wince. I don't even want to drink anymore—I've had way too much already.

I sigh heavily, trying to get him to acknowledge me. When he doesn't, I slam the bottle on the nearby table and stand. This gets his attention, and his eyes track me to the door. "Where the fuck are you going?"

"Home," I reply, pulling the door open.

He's behind me in a second, slamming it closed again. "You drive me fucking insane," he mutters. I turn to face him, trapped between the door and his body. His hands are placed either side of my head. "You're a pain in my arse," he adds.

"No one asked you to keep showing up."

"Yet I do," he says with a sigh. "And I always will."

I scoff. "You'll get fed up with me eventually, Bert."

He shakes his head, gently tucking my hair away from my face. "That's the thing, Red, I don't think I will." His words sit heavy on my heart. I don't dare believe him—men never show up for long. "So, you can keep being a pain in my arse, I'm still gonna be here. Just please stop running out on me, okay? I'll take you home if that's what you want."

He turns to grab his car keys. "I can look after myself," I say quietly because I like the idea of him driving me home, but I can't just tell him that.

"Sure, you can, Red. But I'm a gentleman, so allow me. It makes me feel better."

I bite my lip to hide the smile. "If it makes you feel better, I guess I'll allow it."

I got Meli's text message demanding I go to hers first thing and help her choose an outfit while I was eating breakfast and arguing with Mav. I use it as an excuse to get out the clubhouse before Mav lectures me on attitude and respect. He's still yelling after me as I rush out. I go around to the back of the clubhouse and cut over the small field to where Meli and Arthur's house sits proudly. It's a beautiful building, and the fact it's right on the club's doorstep is a bonus.

I go right into the kitchen, where Arthur's sitting with Albert, looking at the laptop. They both look up, and Arthur rolls his eyes. "You're supposed to knock," he comments.

I grin, knocking on the table as I pass him. "Apologies, Mr. Taylor," I say, my voice dripping with sarcasm.

"Hey, do you know the surname Harrison?" asks Albert.

I shake my head. "Should I?"

He shrugs. "His name keeps coming up. Apparently, he's dealing around the Abbey Road estate."

"I'm starting to think that estate is more trouble than it's worth," I say.

"We can't risk leaving it to the streets like before," says Arthur. "Not after what happened with Jenifer Hall and the Palmer brothers," he adds. They'd run it before, until we took care of them, fitting them up for murder and sending them to prison.

"And Mav doesn't know of him?"

Albert shakes his head. "Which means he's got to be a chancer, right? One of us would have heard of him otherwise."

"Which means he's a nobody and we shouldn't worry," I say.

Albert smirks, grabbing my hand as I try to pass. "We said that before, and I ended up with a price on my head."

I stare down at our joined hands, then I look to Arthur, who's frowning. I pull free and step away, unsure of how to feel about Albert's obvious display of affection. Albert grins. "You going shy on me, Red?"

"You two are a thing?" asks Arthur.

ALBERT

"No," I snap at the same time Albert says yes.

Arthur looks back and forth between us. "Well, which is it, yes or no?"

"It's yes," says Albert before I can reply. "She's having a hard time accepting it."

"Fuck," mutters Arthur in surprise. "Have you told Ma?"

Albert shakes his head. "Not yet."

His brother smirks. "Good luck with that one." His words bother me more than I care to admit. Their mum seems lovely. She's been staying at the clubhouse for a while now, and everyone loves her. Admittedly, I haven't spent much time getting to know her but only because I'm always so busy. But Arthur's right, his mum won't want Albert dating someone like me.

I head upstairs to find Meli, ignoring the inner voice currently shaming me for never being good enough. "What's the urgent matter I had to rush over for?" I ask.

"I need you to fake tan my back, I need help finding a dress for tonight, and . . ." She pauses and sighs. "Do you ever think you're not good enough?" she blurts, flopping down on her bed.

I join her. "What are you talking about?"

She shakes her head. "All the dinner parties, the dressing up so I can chat with boring bastards at dinner parties I don't want to be at, I just feel so out of my depth."

I smile. "Right. You mean you don't feel like you belong?"

"Arthur says I'm being silly. He grew up in Peckham and no one judges him. But it just feels like it's his world, not mine."

"Meli, you're way better than any of those jumped-up fuckers who go to these bullshit things. Stop doubting yourself. You have as much right to be there as anyone."

"I'm terrified I'll say something to embarrass him. There're always women there throwing themselves at him, and I just feel so . . . inadequate."

"You're not. You're amazing. What's the dinner for?"

"Some property development Arthur and Albert are investing in."

"Both of them?" I ask, frowning.

"Yep. And it's a plus one, so I can't really get out of it. Not that Arthur would let me."

I grab her fake tan. "That's because he's proud to have you on his arm." I busy myself pretending to read the label while my mind goes into overdrive. Albert hasn't asked me

ALBERT

to the dinner even though he's insisting we're a thing. It bothers me.

"How about you come?" Meli suggests.

I laugh. "No. No way."

"Come on, please. I can get you on the list if I call Arthur's P.A."

"No. Arthur complains when I come here to see you, if I crash your night, he'll be raging."

She grabs my arm. "Please, Rosey. For me. I'll feel less out of place with you there."

"Great, thanks, because I'm a loser too?"

She laughs. "We're losers together. Broken losers."

My heart aches. She's right. We're both broken because of decisions Eagle made. "I don't have anything to wear or a plus one."

"I have something for you to wear, and bring Archer."

I shake my head. "He's probably busy with work."

"I'll text and ask," she says, grabbing her phone and tapping away.

"I'd feel out of place. Who's Albert taking? Do we know her?" I ask casually.

"Not sure, probably a random hook-up like usual." She smiles at her phone. "He's free. I'll get tickets sorted."

ALBERT

I push my way through the guests until I spot my brothers by the bar. Charlie shakes my hand, and Tommy hands me a drink. "Where's Art?" I ask, glancing around the room. My eyes freeze on Rosey. "What's she doing here?"

"Arthur is showing the plans to Mr. Davies. Who's the 'she' you're referring to?" asks Charlie, looking over the crowd.

"Red."

"Don't you start. We had Arthur bending our ear about it just a second ago. Meli arranged it."

I didn't invite Rosey because I know she hates this sort of thing, but seeing her now, in a long, red dinner dress with a slit up one side to show flashes of her tanned leg and her hair curled and draped over one shoulder, I regret my decision. I head over to her, and when she spots me, she looks annoyed. "Albert."

"Surely, you knew I'd be here, Red, It's my event."

"Meli forced me to come," she mutters.

"I would have invited you if I'd thought you'd say yes."

"Since when has me agreeing or not ever stopped you?"

ALBERT

I grin. "True. I guess I didn't want to make you feel uncomfortable."

She glances around. "Who did you bring? Is she more socially acceptable?"

I frown. "I didn't bring anyone, Red. Why would I when I'm with you?"

She takes a gulp of her drink. "You're free and single, you can bring anyone you want. I don't care."

I let her words sink in. "Hold on, did you bring someone?" Her mouth opens and then closes as Archer joins us, handing Rosey another drink.

"Boss." He nods in greeting.

"Un-fucking-believable," I mutter, walking away.

ROSEY

"What is his problem?" snaps Archer.

I shrug helplessly. I wasn't prepared for him to be here alone. I'd convinced myself he'd have a beautiful date on his arm. One he could show off with pride. "Told you these things were dull," Meli says as she joins us.

"Maybe we should just go," I suggest. "Leave you to it."

"Don't you dare," hisses Meli, grabbing my hand. "I can't get through dinner on my own."

We're led through to another room where large, round tables seat eight. I sit beside Meli, and Archer places his drink down before heading for the bathroom. Albert sits in the seat, ignoring the fact it's reserved for Archer. "It's taken," I mutter.

"By me."

"Look, it wasn't my idea to bring—"

"I don't wanna hear it, Red. Save it for later."

"Later?" I repeat.

Archer returns, standing awkwardly. "You're in my seat," he eventually says.

Albert looks up at him. "It didn't have a name on it. Sit somewhere else."

"But Rosey's my date."

Albert glances at me. "That right, Red? Do you want me to move?"

I fidget uncomfortably. "It's fine, Archer, just sit anywhere," I mutter, and he frowns before taking his drink and sitting beside Tommy.

ALBERT

Dinner is served and I eat in silence while Albert chats with Arthur about business. When desserts come out, I'm stuffed, so I slide it away from me and lean back in my seat. Albert places a hand on my knee, taking advantage of the thigh-high slit. He begins to move farther up my leg and across my inner thigh. I clamp my legs closed before he can get that far, and he smirks. "Make me force them open," he whispers, "and everyone at this table, including your date, will know what I'm doing under here."

"It's not appropriate," I whisper-hiss. He pinches my thigh, and I yelp, causing Meli to look at me. I smile awkwardly, parting my legs and allowing Albert to slip his hand into my knickers.

"You're acting so weird tonight," she says. "What's wrong with you?"

"Nothing," I say defensively. "I've got stomach cramps."

"I was wondering if you wanted to come over to my place tomorrow night. I've got the kids for Mav so he and Rylee can have a date night."

Albert presses his finger to my clit, and I sit straighter. "Erm, not really my thing," I say.

"Or mine, but I'm being a good aunt."

His finger slides into me, and I bite my lip. "I have work anyway."

"It's weird you plan your work. Shouldn't you just do it when the opportunity arises?"

"I like to be organised," I almost whisper as Albert moves his fingers faster. He's chatting with Arthur completely normal, as if his fingers aren't buried inside me, and just as I begin to feel the delicious warm feeling, he withdraws them, popping them into his mouth and licking them clean. I stare open-mouthed, wondering how the hell no one saw any of that. He then swipes his fingers through my melting ice cream and places them to my lips. I hesitate, and he arches a brow until I open and take them into my mouth.

"What the fuck?" asks Meli.

"Didn't she mention us?" asks Albert.

"No, she bloody didn't," says Meli, sounding outraged. "Bathroom, now."

I follow her to avoid a scene. The second we enter the bathroom, she spins to face me. "You and Albert?" she screeches. "Since when?"

"It's not a thing," I say. "He thinks it's a thing, but it isn't."

"You just sucked dessert from his fingers, don't tell me it's not a thing."

"It's sex," I say, shrugging.

"It's a thing," she says firmly. "I can see it in your eyes."

I sigh, rubbing my hands over my face as I sit on the velvet seating inside the bathroom. "He's going to break me," I admit, "but he won't leave me be."

She joins me, looking concerned. "Why didn't you tell me?"

"Because I can't admit he might actually be having an impact on me."

Meli smiles. "This is so exciting."

"No. No, it isn't, Meli. I just want him to stop, but he won't. He shows up where I am. He does things to me that I never let anyone do—"

"Like?" she asks, sitting up for the gossip.

"Like he bosses me around."

She frowns. "That's not exciting."

"He doesn't take my bullshit, Meli. He'll call me out on it and then shut me up with an order or a kiss or something else that just stops me in my tracks and I . . ." I take a few breaths. My chest is tight and my vision blurs.

"Shit, are you having a panic attack?" Meli asks, taking my hands. She grabs a paper bag from beside the sink and gives it to me. "It's a sanitary bag, but it's clean." I press it to my mouth and breathe in and out slowly like she instructs. "Just relax. This isn't as scary as you think." I roll my eyes. She has no idea. "Shit, and you brought Archer to this dinner as your date." I nod. "He must have been raging," she says with a laugh.

I feel a little calmer, so I remove the bag from my face. "Since Eagle, I haven't felt anything for anyone. And what I felt for him wasn't anything good, so I guess this is the first time since Maverick that I've liked someone."

"You've not felt for anyone since you were a teenager?" she asks, and I shake my head. "Rosey, that's so sad."

"Pathetic," I mutter.

"No, not at all. It's your turn to find happiness. Grab it with both hands."

"I have so much to deal with," I protest.

"Bullshit. Make this happen, Rosey, or you'll regret it forever."

"But Ollie is so unsettled and—"

"It's just excuses. Ollie is a teenage boy. He'll survive without you breathing down his neck, trust me. Besides,

ALBERT

Albert would make a good stepdad." She laughs, and I smile.

"I just don't think I'm ready to jump in, yah know?"

"You can't avoid all relationships just in case they turn out to be arseholes who hurt you. Heartbreak is how we learn. Have some fun. See how it goes."

"I know if this progresses, he'll start asking questions about Eagle and what happened. I don't want him to see me like that," I admit.

"I get it," she says simply. "You know, I felt the exact same with Arthur. But it wasn't as bad as I'd made myself believe. Once I told him what happened to me, he didn't look at me any different. Albert isn't going to judge you on your past, a past you couldn't help, and you can't keep everyone at arm's length just so you don't have to talk about it." She smiles. "I should have guessed. You were so quiet tonight, it's not like you at all. Could he be the man to tame you?" she teases.

I roll my eyes. "I don't think so. We should go back before Arthur sends out a search party."

As the words leave my mouth, the door opens and Arthur steps in, grinning at Meli. "No, Art, not here," she hisses.

"Yes, here," he says, moving towards her.

She stands, backing away and glancing around helplessly. "Can't you just wait until we get home?"

He guides her into a cubicle and slams the door. "I guess that's my hint to go," I mutter, leaving them to it.

I head outside in the hope I'll flag a cab, but Albert is already out there. He holds up his car keys. "I thought you'd try and escape."

"It's early," I say. "I can get a cab."

He shakes his head. "Not happening." He takes my hand in his and leads me to the car park. "You pissed me off tonight, Red," he says, staring straight ahead. "Don't do that shit again."

We get in the car, and he drives us in the direction towards his place. I stay quiet, allowing myself to enjoy one night of normal.

The second we're in the door, he's on me, slamming me against the wall and pulling my dress to my waist. He drops to his knees and snaps the thin material of my knickers, letting them fall to the floor before burying his head between my legs.

Chapter Nine

ALBERT

Rosey is quiet as we shower together. She tried to insist she shower alone, but I'm still annoyed about her little date and I'm not ready to let her out my sight. "I never thought I'd hear myself say this, Red, but I miss your backchat. What's wrong?"

As if I interrupted her daydream, she shakes her head slightly and looks at me in surprise. "Huh?"

I turn the shower off and grab us each a towel. "What's wrong?"

"Nothing," she says, wrapping herself up and moving past me to escape to the bedroom.

"I may not be the expert on relationships, but I know when a woman says nothing is wrong, it usually means there's something very wrong."

"Why am I here, Albert?" she asks suddenly. I follow her through to the bedroom. "Why did you bring me here instead of taking me home?"

I frown. "Isn't it clear, Red?" She shakes her head. "Cos I wanna be with you."

She sits on the edge of the bed, placing her hands either side of her and ducking her chin down to avoid eye contact. "Why?"

"Why do I want to be with you?" She nods. "Because I like you."

"You like having sex with me?"

I almost smile before realising she's serious. "Yes, Red, of course, I do, but that's not what I meant. I like you. A lot."

Her head jerks up. "Why?" she asks again.

This time, a small laugh escapes me. "You want a list or something?" She doesn't reply, her eyes burning into me with something I can't quite recognise . . . fear, maybe. I move closer, until I'm standing in front of her and she has to look up to keep eye contact. "The list is huge, Red, from the way you give me grief every second I'm with you, to the way you love those closest to you with a fierceness I only see in my brother. I love the way you laugh and the way you can take a man down with words. I love your green eyes and how pink your lips are." I rub my thumb over her lower lip as I say the words. "Everything about you sets me on fire."

"I don't know how to do this," she whispers. "I've never had this."

"You've never had a man interested in you? I find that impossible to believe, Red. Every man who passes you stares longingly."

She slowly shakes her head. "Never anyone I've wanted to."

I gently take her chin in my fingers and tip her head back as I press my lips to hers. "I know you're finding it hard, Rosey. I get it. But I'm a patient man, and I already know it's gonna take that to keep you. We're doing this at your pace."

"Doing what?" she asks. Her vulnerability shows in her eyes again, and I press a kiss to her forehead.

"Us, Red. We're doing us. Me and you. No more dates with fuck boy or I'll kill him," I say. Archer's gotten away with far too much as it is, and the only reason he's still breathing right now is because of her. I gently push her to lie back, bracing myself over her on my elbows. "Who do you belong with, Red?" I whisper, kissing along her collar bone as I remove her towel. When she doesn't reply, I glance up and see she's smirking. "Don't test me," I warn.

"You," she whispers, raking her fingers through my hair as I work my mouth down her chest.

I spent hours worshipping Rosey's body, making love. Something both of us are new to. And as I lay beside her, I wonder if it's too soon to do it all over again. She tuns on her side, wrapping a sheet around herself and smiling at me shyly. I've never seen this side to her, and I love it. "If this doesn't work out, how will it end?" she asks.

I arch a brow. "Why're you talking like that, Red? I only just got you to agree, and now you're thinking about the end?"

She smiles wider. "I've never been dumped before. I don't know how I'll handle it."

"Knowing you, with a knife and some harsh words."

"Doesn't that worry you?"

I grin, turning onto my side to face her. "Should it?"

Her mind goes somewhere else and the smile fades. "The last man who hurt me ended up dead."

"Eagle?" I guess, and she nods. "It was a different kind of hurt, Red. He deserved to die."

"I don't think we should tell anyone just yet," she mutters. "About this."

I laugh. There's no way I'm keeping us quiet. "You're gonna tell Ollie, and then we're official. I'll tell the whole damn world."

"I mean it," she says more seriously now. "Ollie's going through some stuff and I—"

"Need help?" I finish for her, and she scowls. "It's okay to admit it, Red. I wanna be part of your life and with that comes Ollie. I get that."

She pushes to sit up. "I don't need help," she snaps. "I'm doing just fine."

"I know you are. But won't it be easier to have someone to lean on?"

She rubs the back of her neck. "Jesus," she mutters, "suddenly you want to play dad?"

"That's not what I meant, Rosey. I'll have as little or as much input as you want me to have. You're doing great with Ollie. I just meant I'll be there for you." I pull her to lay back down, and she allows me to. I throw my leg over her and tuck her against me. "Stop looking for reasons to fight so you can get out of here. Pushing me away isn't an option anymore because I'm not going anywhere."

"Until one day you do," she mutters, her eyes briefly flicking to mine.

I wrap my arms around her tighter and kiss her shoulder. "Not happening."

"I don't want Ollie to know just yet. Not until I'm certain."

I roll my eyes, even though she can't see me. She's convinced I'm not sticking around, and it doesn't matter how many times I say it, she'll always be waiting for me to leave. "Fine. If you want to go slow, I get it. We'll tell him when you're ready."

Arthur grins the second I step into my office the next day. "You're a crazy bastard," he tells me, laughing.

"I assume you mean because I like Rosey?"

ALBERT

"I suspected you were fucking, Bert, but you're actually seeing her? Jesus, don't you like your balls attached?"

"Just keep it to yourself for now. She doesn't want to tell Ollie."

"Speaking of Ollie," he says carefully, "he's involved with a few names on our books."

I frown. "What do you mean?"

"Dave Blain?" I nod, recognising the name as one of our top earners. "Ollie hangs out with his younger brother, Steven."

I shrug. "So?"

"Come on, Bert, don't act dumb. You were right. How many of our guys have their brothers running too?"

"Doesn't mean Ollie is. But I'll speak with Dave. How did you find out?"

"I saw him on the Abbey Road estate. He was with a big crowd. Should I speak to Rosey about it?"

I shake my head. This is my chance to show her I'm serious. "I'll keep an eye on it and instruct Dave on the situation."

Arthur smirks. "You're gonna try and sort this behind her back?"

"She's got a lot on. She doesn't need the worry."

He holds his hands up in surrender. "You know what you're doing. I just think giving her the heads up might go better than you keeping it from her."

"I'm not keeping it from her. We don't know anything. He could just be hanging out with them. It doesn't mean he's dealing."

I turn into the Abbey Road estate and the gangs of youths immediately turn to watch as my car slows to a stop outside the flats where Dave Blain runs his business from. I call to tell him I've arrived, and minutes later, he appears, jogging over to the car. He climbs into the passenger side. "What's up, boss?"

"You know we don't run kids, right?" I say, and he visibly swallows.

"'Course."

"How old's Steven?"

"Boss, I don't run my brother on the streets," he says, frowning. "I swear it."

"What about his mate, Ollie?"

"Fuck no."

ALBERT

"He's been seen hanging out round here, Dave."

"Cos he's with Ste, but he ain't part of what's going on. He just hangs out with the group."

"Is he part of any gangs?"

He shrugs. "Not mine."

"If I find out you're lying, I'll come back for you."

"I'm not. He's just a kid who hangs out with my brother, boss. You want me to keep an eye on him?"

I nod. "Yeah, but don't give the game away." He nods, slipping out the car. I believe him. I trust the circle we're building on this estate.

ROSEY

I arranged to meet my mum in a café not far from her place. When she arrives, she looks tired and she's walking like she's hurt. She spots me and heads over to the table at the back of the place, wincing as she lowers into the seat. "You're hurt," I state, and she waves me away like it's nothing. "I got you a black coffee like you used to drink it," I point out, nodding to the cup.

She wraps her hands around the mug. "Thanks."

"So, what's happening in your life?" I ask.

She leans back in the chair, glancing around and picking the dry skin around her nails. "Same old."

I stare past her, watching an elderly couple. They're not speaking at all, but they look comfortable together, more so than Mum and me right now. "Are you back in London for good?"

She nods. "You went back to the MC," she adds. "I never thought you'd go back there."

"Eagle's gone. The club's better for it. I didn't see the point in staying away."

"And Ollie, how's he fitting in?"

"Fine. Mav's giving him things to do around the place. He's helping fix bikes in the garage some days." The conversation feels forced, and I begin to wonder why I bothered. We have nothing to say anymore.

"I'd like to meet him again, get to know him."

I frown. "Why?" She was never the nurturing type, and after I had Ollie, she couldn't have been less interested. I don't even remember her holding him.

"He's my grandson," she states, like that's the only explanation she needs to give.

I frown. "I'm your daughter and you never gave a shit about me, so what's changed?"

ALBERT

"That's not fair, Rose."

I shudder, only she and Eagle used to call me by my birth name. "It's Rosey," I correct.

"I know I wasn't the best mum," I scoff, and she takes a breath, "but I'd like to try and be a better grandmother."

I feel the tension building in my jaw and I clench my hands under the table. "He doesn't need you," I mutter.

"I'm his only other blood relative."

"Not true," I snap. "He's got Mav, Meli, Hadley, and Bea."

"Bea," she repeats, laughing. "What is she to him? His stepmother?"

I resent her tone and sit straighter. "She treats him like her grandson. They have a good relationship."

"But she isn't that, is she? Her husband knocked you up, so Ollie is the love child of her husband." She laughs again, and it reminds me of when I was little and she'd sneer at me with contempt.

"Is that why you wanted to meet?" I ask, trying to sound calmer than I am. "To rake up old ground?"

There's a tightness to her eyes as she responds. "What's the point? You did what you did, and now, we're here so . . ."

I press my fingers to my temples and briefly close my eyes. "Oh my god, you still blame me for everything, don't you?"

"We're going around in circles. I don't want to argue with you, Rose. Too much has happened, and I'd like to get to know you and Ollie again. Let's draw a line under it all."

I pick at the menu, letting her words sink in. "Not until you say it," I mutter, glancing at her. "Tell me it wasn't my fault."

She sits straighter, jutting out her judgemental chin and pressing her lips together in a firm line. "You want me to lie?"

I slam my hand on the table, taking us both by surprise. "No," I hiss, "I want you to see that I was just a kid. I want you to admit that I had a shit mum who taught me that my body was only good for one thing. I want you to tell me it wasn't my fault that a man three times my age came into my bed and that you let him."

She looks astounded, almost lost for words, as her mouth opens and closes like a goldfish. "We clearly see the past through very different eyes."

ALBERT

"So, you didn't tell me to keep my mouth shut and accept it?"

She shakes her head. "Of course not."

Angry tears spring to my eyes. "Liar," I whisper. "I remember," I add. "You were there."

"When Crow took what was his, I was there. We were all there."

I shake my head, a stray tear slipping down my cheek. I swipe it away angrily. "No, you were there," I tell her. "And Crow and Eagle and Ripper. I remember it, Mum. I remember it all."

"And so do I," she snaps, leaning closer. "And I remember how you spread your damn legs like the whore I taught you to be." She glances around to make sure no one is paying attention and it causes another childhood flashback as I stare at her pinched features. "We had a job in that club, that was it. Have sex and keep the men happy. No one had a free ride, Rose. Not even you."

"I was a kid," I whisper, more tears falling. I don't remember the last time I cried, and the feeling makes me sick to my stomach.

"I did you a favour," she says more calmly. "They were going to take you eventually, anyway, so I stayed with you."

I almost choke on my tears. "You think you were being a good mum?" I ask. "Staying by my side while they *raped* me?"

"It wasn't rape, Rose. Crow won the fight, and you were the prize."

"I never agreed to be the damn prize," I cry, and people turn to see what the commotion is. I wipe my eyes again. "I shouldn't have agreed to this," I mutter, pushing to stand. "Stay away from me and Ollie."

I step into the fresh air and take some deep breaths. I usually avoid emotion and situations that make me lose it, and between Mum, Ollie, and Albert, I feel my life is spiralling. Taking a seat on a nearby wall, I close my eyes, letting the sun warm my face. I remember the night Eagle ordered Mav and his half-brother, Crow, to fight, announcing the winner would get my virginity. I remember his delighted expression when Mav stormed out after punching Crow. Technically, Mav won, but that's not how Eagle or Crow saw it. They said Mav walking out didn't make him the winner, so they took what they wanted against my will while Mum stroked my hair and whispered encouraging words. I shake away the image and re-open my eyes. It's in the past, where it belongs. I've moved on.

ALBERT

Glancing around, my eyes stop on Albert's car parked across the street in the hotel car park. I frown, wondering why he would be in a cheap hotel. I pull out my mobile and send him a text asking how his day is and what he's up to.

Minutes later, he replies.

Albert: Day's going good. You? I'm in back to back meetings at the office all day. Dinner later?

I bite the inside of my lip, staring at the text. *Why would he lie to me?* Before my mind runs away with me, I call Meli. "Hey," she answers brightly. "How did it go with your mum?"

"Terrible," I reply, "which is why I'm calling. I need you to rationalise something before I overthink and go crazy."

"Okay?"

"Albert's car is in the car park beside the East Hotel."

"Right."

"So, I text asking how his day was and what he was up to. He lied. He said he's in back-to-back meetings at the office."

"Rosey, he'll probably head there next. He moves around a lot."

"To cheap hotels?" I ask. "It's not his usual meeting spot."

"No. True. Doesn't mean anything, though. Maybe a client arranged the meeting place."

I nod, even though she can't see me. It's a plausible explanation. "I'm going in to take a closer look."

"That's probably not a good idea, Rosey. You've had a difficult morning with your mum, for one, you're not thinking straight. Plus, what if he's with a very important client and you cause a scene? Come back to the clubhouse and we'll talk about it."

Another text beeps through, and I glance at my phone.

Albert: *I'll be at the office until at least seven. I can pick you up at eight?*

"I have to go," I tell Meli, disconnecting the call.

I cross the road and head inside. There's a small reception area with a man behind the desk. "How can I help?" he greets.

"I'm here for a meeting with Mr. Taylor."

He checks his book and nods. "He's in room 5 just along the corridor," he tells me, and my heart beats faster.

"Not the bar?" I ask, hoping he has it wrong.

ALBERT

He shakes his head. "Ms. Spencer has already arrived. Would you like me to call the room to announce your arrival?"

I shake my head. "No. They're expecting me."

I stand outside the door listening but hear nothing. I take a deep breath and knock. "Room service," I announce.

A minute later, the door is ripped open and Albert scowls, his face softening when he sees it's me. I take in his appearance. He doesn't look just fucked, but he's missing his jacket and tie. "Rosey," he says, sounding confused.

"I saw your car," I say as way of explanation.

His smile is perplexed. "I told you I'm in meetings all day."

"In your office," I point out, "but this doesn't look like your office, Bert." I arch a brow, waiting for him to rush and explain with another lie.

"We should do this later," he says, his voice firm.

It only adds to my suspicions. "I think we'll do it now," I snap, shoving the door open. He steps aside, sighing heavily as I pass him. There's no one else in the room, and my eyes fall to the bathroom door, which is closed. "Is she in there?"

"You're acting crazy," he whispers.

"I thought you like that about me," I say sarcastically before banging on the bathroom door. "Come out," I demand.

"Rosey, it's not what you think," he snaps. "I'm in a meeting."

"In a seedy hotel that rents rooms by the hour," I snap.

The bathroom door opens, and a woman appears looking confused. "Albert?" she asks, looking to him for answers.

"Sorry about this, Lauren. She's my—"

"No, I'm not," I snap before he can label me. "Not anymore."

I leave the room, slamming the door behind me. I hear Albert let out a stream of curses before the door's ripped open. "Rosey," he growls, but I march faster. "Rosey, stop now."

"Get back to your meeting," I yell over my shoulder.

I hear his footsteps chasing me down, and the urge to run is overwhelming, but I force myself to remain calm. "Jesus, Red, stop fucking running and listen to me," he orders. I break out into the street. "Rosey," he yells, and people turn to stare.

ALBERT

"I knew you'd do it," I snap.

His arms go around my waist, and I fight him until I break free. "Just calm down," he growls. "I haven't done anything."

"Yet. I'm not stupid."

"You're acting pretty stupid to me," he mutters.

I turn to walk away, and he apologises immediately. "Okay, sorry. Just hear me out. I really am in a meeting." I slow, folding my arms over my chest and staring down at the ground. "I know it's easier for you to believe I'm up to no good. Then you can walk away and this torrent of emotion you feel can stop. You can shut it down. But I'm not cheating on you, Red. I'm not. She's my last meeting here before I have to go to the office for the rest of my appointments. I didn't tell you where I was because it was irrelevant. Had you asked what I was doing here, I would have told you."

"Who is she?" I mutter.

He risks stepping closer. "Your next job," he says, gently stroking a thumb over my cheek. "She needs a contract carried out."

"Why the hotel?"

"You know I can't do this shit in the open, Red. I can't be seen with her."

"I saw my mum," I mutter, like that explains my irrational behaviour.

"Why didn't you tell me you were meeting her? I would have cleared my diary."

My heart squeezes slightly. *He would have cancelled everything to be with me.* "I feel like an idiot," I whisper.

He cups my face in his hands, lifting until I meet his eyes. "Go to my place. I'll cook us dinner, and you can tell me about your mum."

"Ollie," I mutter. "I should be home."

He looks disappointed but nods anyway. "Okay. Fit me in tomorrow?" I nod, and he gently kisses me on the lips. "I'll call you tonight."

Chapter Ten

ALBERT

I watch Rosey walk away. She was rattled when she turned up at the hotel, and now, she looks beaten and exhausted. I didn't think she'd be in this end of town, and I could kick myself for the misjudgement.

I head back to the room where Lauren Spencer waits patiently. "Sorted?" she asks.

I nod and open the file on the bed. "Everything you need is in this file," I tell her. She stands closer, staring at Archer's photograph. "You keep Rosey out of it," I add.

She smiles. "I intend to. She's a firecracker."

"If she sees you, she'll know instantly, and the deal will be off."

She takes the file and sighs. "Got it. And you're happy with her, Bert?" She bites on her lower lip suggestively, and I grin, nodding.

"Very happy."

She heads for the door. "I remember you used to say the same about me."

I'm back at the office when Dave calls. "Boss," he says when I answer, "I don't know if this is relevant, but I keep hearing the name Dougie Harrison. Ollie mentioned it earlier to Ste. Said he's gonna take on the estate."

"What does that mean?"

"He's moving gear, boss."

"And how does Ollie know that?"

"Not sure. I didn't push in case he got spooked. He seems to know him pretty well, though."

"Thanks." I disconnect and scrub my hands over my tired face. *What the fuck is Ollie mixed up in?*

When I finally walk through my door at nine that evening, I'm surprised to find Rosey waiting for me in the

ALBERT

hall wearing nothing but her knickers. I smirk. "Thank god I didn't bring a client back."

"I figured you'd had a hard day and I didn't help with my hysteria."

I laugh. "And what happened to Ollie?"

She shrugs. "He had plans and I didn't want to stick around the clubhouse cos Meli would have forced me to help her babysit."

I shrug out of my jacket and sweep her against me. Backing her into the living room, I bend her over the couch. "It's gonna be fast and hard," I warn her, pulling her knickers to one side.

Rosey returns from the shower and takes a seat at the kitchen island. She watches as I prepare dinner. "You cook?" she muses.

"I learnt young," I tell her, stirring the bolognaise. "Mum was working all the hours she could, and Art was out making us a name. Someone had to watch the brats."

She smiles. "You were a good brother."

"Not sure Tommy and Charlie would agree," I joke, "but I tried my best."

"It's all we can do," she says, and I feel like she's referring to her situation with Ollie.

"What plans did Ollie have?"

She shrugs. "He was seeing his friends."

I nod. "Do you know them?"

"Some."

"I remember having to check on Charlie. He always attracted the wrong sort of friends."

"Really?" she asks.

"I got him out of some scrapes," I say, smirking. "Ma still doesn't know half the shit he got up to."

"He was lucky to have you to rescue him."

"Do you think you'd want more kids? Someone for Ollie to guide through life?"

She laughs. "No. That ship sailed long ago. I never wanted kids."

"Yet you had Ollie?"

"I was young. I didn't know I was pregnant until really late, and by then, it was too late to terminate. Mum was furious, so I decided to keep him, more as fuck you to her, but actually, it backfired because she left and I had to deal with him alone."

I lean on the counter. "That was a shitty decision on her part. Why didn't she take you with her?"

"She was never a good mum. Me having a child was too hard for her to deal with, and basically, she couldn't be arsed to make the effort."

"But you did it alone anyway, that shows courage."

"Or stupidity."

"How did you manage it?" I ask, checking the pot of boiling spaghetti.

"Day by day," she mutters, shifting uncomfortably. "Coming back to the club was the best thing I ever did, though. It made life easier, and I could work knowing Ollie was taken care of."

"How did you get into your role?" I ask, grabbing two dishes from the cupboard.

Her eyes light up again. "I met a guy," she begins, and I scowl. "Nothing like that. But he gave me self-defence lessons. I was good at something finally. It gave me some power back and I became a better version of myself. I stood up to Eagle, first of all, and when he began to back off, I realised I wasn't weak like before. I trained hard—self-defence, boxing, anything I could to make me stronger. One night, I was in a bar watching a couple argue. He dragged her out back for a beating, and I followed. He struck her once, and I made sure he'd never do it again. Each time I got involved in some sort of dispute, I felt better about myself. Before long, I was getting hired to do it."

"You come alive when you talk about work," I say.

"It's the only stable thing in my life."

I spoon spaghetti onto the dishes. "Not anymore, Red. Not anymore." Because now, she has me.

Once I've dished up and we're at the table, I pour her a glass of wine. "How did it go with your mum?"

"Badly," she admits, twisting her fork into the spaghetti. "I don't know why I bothered to see her. I knew how it would go."

"Does she know about what happened with Eagle and how he died?"

She shakes her head. "She knows nothing about my life now. The last time I saw her, she was getting on a bus to Ireland. Ollie was a baby."

"Were you guys ever close?"

She tastes the bolognaise and closes her eyes in appreciation. "This is good," she says through a mouthful, and I smile. I've never really cooked for anyone but Ma or my brothers. "No, not really. She's not the maternal type."

"So, how come it didn't go well?"

"Tell me about your meeting today, the one I crashed," she asks, changing the subject.

"Not much to tell," I say, shrugging.

"Why's she hiring?"

"I don't know that she is for definite. She was putting out the feelers."

Rosey frowns. "You met someone who isn't sure if they want to hire a hit?" she asks sceptically.

I backtrack, realising my mistake. We'd never meet anyone face to face unless we were certain it was going ahead. "I mean, after your little show, it made her nervous. I might have to pass it to Archer."

She looks away, embarrassed, and I feel bad for the lie. "Any plans to see your mum again?"

She shakes her head. "Tell me about your past."

"Not much to tell."

"Bullshit. You grew up with Arthur Taylor, there has to be stories there. What about dating and kids?" She's smiling again, and I'm relieved she isn't hanging on to the details of earlier.

"No kids. I don't want them. Didn't have time to date, Art made sure of that. And my childhood was a good one."

"Why are you holding out on me?" she asks, her eyes narrowed playfully.

I sigh. "I'm not. Ma worked hard to raise us alone. She did good. Arthur saw an opportunity to get us some money because Ma struggled with four hungry boys, and the rest is history."

"I only ever knew club life," she offers. "I don't remember a time when it was ever just me and Mum. There was always some guy or a club. She'd work her way through it, and then we'd move again. When she found The Perished Riders, it was the first time we'd settled properly. We had our own rooms and there were kids my age. It was nice . . . for a while."

"What changed?" I ask.

She shrugs, inhaling sharply. "Life, I guess. I'm stuffed. Thanks for dinner, it was amazing." She pushes her half-eaten dinner away. "I should go."

"Where?" I ask.

"Home."

"Stay." It slips out before I can stop it.

She half laughs. "Why? We've had dinner, we did the sex." She stands, and I resist the urge to yell, because for once, it'd be nice not to have to convince her to do what I know deep down she wants to do.

My mobile rings, and she glances at the screen seeing as it's nearest her on the kitchen worktop. She arches a brow. "Lauren," she says.

I shrug. "I'll call her back."

She picks up my phone and hands it to me. "Take it," she says firmly.

I cancel the call. "I'll call her when I'm working."

"Bert, you're a gangster, you're always working. Call her back."

"I'm not doing this with you, Rosey," I snap, frustration evident in my voice. "She probably wants to cancel the hit anyway."

"How did you meet her?" she asks.

"I thought you wanted to go home?"

She taps her fingers on the tabletop. "Have you known her long?"

"I told you earlier, she hired us, I don't know her at all."

Rosey narrows her eyes again. "Who told her about you? I thought you had people to do the meets for that sort of thing. Why are you taking a risk to meet her face to face?"

I sigh heavily. "I'm not doing it, Rosey. Go home."

She shrugs. "Fine, I'll find out myself." She heads for the door, and I groan aloud.

As she reaches it, her mobile rings, but she closes the door before I find out if she bothered to answer.

ROSEY

"Archer?"

"Rosey," he whispers, "I need your help." His voice is shaky, uncertain even, and my heart rate immediately picks up.

"Send me your location, I'll be there," I say.

"I don't know where I am, that's the problem, and I don't have my smart phone, just the burner."

The door to Albert's house opens and he grips my arm, pulling me back inside and slamming it closed. "Bert, not now, I gotta go," I tell him. He takes the mobile from me and disconnects the call. "What the fuck?"

"You can't go to him," he says firmly. "It's too late."

ALBERT

Something about the seriousness in his face makes my stomach lurch. "What are you talking about? What have you done?" He moves back into the kitchen, and I follow. I'm not used to feeling so panicked and it causes a nauseous feeling in my stomach. "Albert?" I push, my tone serious.

"He was a liability and a threat to me. I tried to keep him alive for your sake but . . ."

I stare wide-eyed. "But what?"

"But it wasn't working."

My throat tightens and I instinctively rub my neck to try and ease it. "You hired a hit on him?"

"Don't get sentimental on me, it's business." I glance around as rage replaces anything else I'm currently feeling. He gives an easy grin, trying to work out my next move. "Let's not do anything crazy, Red." He carefully takes the knife he was using to chop vegetables earlier and places it in the sink out of my reach. "Look, you wanted to retire, I've found someone to replace you, so I don't need Archer. And keeping him alive would have caused me grief down the line."

I take deep breaths, wiping my now sweaty palms down my jeans. "Give me back my phone," I mutter.

"I've already given the word," he tells me, placing my phone in my waiting hand. "It's too late."

"Pray I don't get to Lauren before she ends his life, or you'll be needing yet another replacement."

He gives me a warning glare. "Don't go against me, Red. It's not worth it."

"Because you'll kill me?" I ask, arching a brow.

"Maverick signed off on this too. We were all in agreement."

I slam my hand on the kitchen worktop angrily. "I wasn't," I yell. "You didn't even bother to fucking consult me."

"Because I knew you were too close. You're not thinking with your head."

I back away. Tears are threatening to fall, and I can't let him see me like that. "Stay the hell away from me."

"Rosey, don't be like that. Business and what we do privately are two very different things."

I scoff. "Fuck you, Albert. Fuck you, fuck your brother, fuck your whole damn family. You come near me again and I'll make you my final kill." It's dangerous to threaten him, but I'm angry and . . . and I'm fucking hurting. The realisation makes me angrier, and I head for the door.

ALBERT

Outside, I try to call the burner phone back, but it rings out. I cry out in frustration. A minute later, Ollie calls me. I take a calming breath and accept his call. "Hey," I say lightly.

"Why didn't you tell me Grandma wanted to see me?" he shouts.

I groan. This is all I need. "What are you talking about?"

"I've just been with her. She was so upset that you told her she can't see me."

I frown. "How the hell have you been with her, you don't even know what she looks like."

"That's all you have to say?" he cries. "You can't stop me."

"I'll come home, and we can talk about it. I just have to find—"

"Don't bother, I'm not there, and I won't be there later either. I'm staying at my friend's house. I can't stand to be around you right now."

"Ollie," I snap, "don't you—" It's too late, he's disconnected the call. I crouch low, holding my head in my hands and fighting back tears.

I take a deep breath and square my shoulders before rising to my feet again. I don't want to call Mav. He agreed to Albert's plan and didn't bother to give me the heads up, so I can't trust him. I decide to call my ex-handler. If I'm gonna find Archer, she might be able to help. I'll deal with Ollie later.

"Long time no see," she answers. "Business or pleasure?"

"Business."

"Oakfield Hotel. Rooftop. Ten minutes." She disconnects, and I head for the hotel.

Oksana Babaev is waiting patiently on the rooftop as arranged. I'm convinced she has underground tunnels to get her to any location in London within ten minutes, no matter where she is. She stands elegantly with a drink in one hand and a cigarette in the other. Her minders are dotted around the place, but they blend into the background well. "Darling, you look tired," she greets me. Her Russian accent is strong, even though she's been in the U.K. for many years.

"In case you knew him, Archer Rose is dead, or at least he will be if I don't find him soon." She has the best poker face and gives me nothing as she takes a sip of her drink.

ALBERT

I wouldn't know anyone on her books, but that's part of the world we live in. They don't buddy us up and privacy is key in this game, but if a hit is happening in London, I'd bet my life she'll know about it. "A woman named Lauren, blonde, my age . . . maybe."

She smiles. "Why are you here, Rosey?"

"I need to save him, Oksana."

"And you thought I could help with that?"

"I thought after years of my dedication to you—"

"How is work going with the Taylor brothers?" she cuts in, letting me know she knows my business and pointing out it's no longer with her. "Are they keeping you busy?"

"We shouldn't be turning on each other," I mutter. "This game is ugly enough without killing one another."

"The game is the game, Rosey. You know I can't give you details. Besides, if Albert Taylor needs a job done, he wouldn't come through me. He has his own connections. His own abandoned warehouses . . ." She trails off, smirking as she turns away. "Enjoy the rest of the evening." It's enough information for me to start with, and I smile as I head for the exit. "And Rosey," she adds, so I turn back, "if you ever need more than what the Taylors can offer, you know where to find me."

The Taylor's own a lot of warehouses. Most are run as factories where Arthur employs women the club help to support after escaping abusive situations. I mentally run through the ones I know of before coming up with two that run alongside the docks and are definitely not used for factories. I leave my car parked down the road and walk to the docks. I don't need to be seen in the area where Archer might be. Slipping under a broken chain fence, I head for the first warehouse. It's securely locked up with no way of getting in unless I break the chains, so I head for the second. As I get closer, I see two motorbikes. The warehouse door is unlocked, and a sliver of dim light shines inside. I move closer and listen. I can hear Maverick's voice, so I step inside, not bothering to sneak around. Mav is standing beside Grim and they're staring down at Archer's lifeless body. I inhale sharply and Grim spins to face me, drawing his gun. When he sees it's me, he lowers it. "Jesus, Rosey, don't sneak around like that."

Mav also turns, his expression guarded. "Rosey . . ."

I ignore them both and rush to where Archer is. There's blood surrounding him, and I drop to my knees, not bothering to hide my emotion as I hold my hands over the wound in his head, unsure of what to do to stop the bleeding. I'm pulled back and I fall on my arse. "Have you lost your fucking mind?" growls Grim. "You can't touch him."

I bury my face in my hands and sob. Huge, body racking sobs. I can't hold it in anymore, because despite everything, I liked Archer. The men stay silent, and after a few minutes, I begin to wipe my face. I stand, and they're both looking uncomfortable, waiting for me to say something. Instead, I head for the exit.

Mav chases me down, taking my arm gently to stop me. "Rosey?" I keep my back to him, knowing if I face him, I'll say something that'll hurt us both. "Did Albert tell you?"

I scowl, turning to face him. "What does it matter, Mav? The real question is, why the hell didn't you tell me?"

"It was the right decision," he continues, ignoring me. "You can't pick and choose when it's right just because you liked the guy."

"I made a deal with him," I snap. "And unlike you shitheads, I keep my deals."

"Look, you're upset, I get it. Take some time and we'll talk about it."

"Who's Lauren? How did she and Albert meet?"

He shrugs. "Old friends apparently."

I nod, angry that Albert also lied to me about that too. "Of course, they are. So, I guess my services aren't required anymore?"

"You wanted to step away and spend time with Ollie, right? He needs you more than the Taylor's or the club."

"I'm taking Ollie away for a while," I announce, making the decision moments ago. I begin to walk away again, and he follows.

"Where?"

"I don't know. Far away from here."

"Rosey, come on, just think about it. You need support with Ollie right now. He's going off the rails and—"

"Wow, that's what you really think? You told me to relax, that he was just being a teenager."

"He is, but there's a danger he's going off the rails. You see it yourself."

"No, Mav, what I see is history repeating itself. This club only cares about the men in it and the women they're fucking. It doesn't matter that I dedicate myself to you or

ALBERT

the MC. It doesn't matter I gave birth to your half-brother. All you care about is the patched members and their ol' ladies."

"That's not true."

"I was and always will be seen as the daughter of a club whore. That's why you don't give a shit about me or Ollie."

"Why do I feel like there's more you're not saying?" he snaps. "You wanna get it all off your chest, Rosey?"

I spin back to him. "Maybe I should, Mav. Maybe we should go over the night you abandoned me and left me to fight off your other half-brother."

"Crow is in the past. We put him in the ground for that shit," he yells.

"*I* put him in the ground," I scream, shoving him hard. He doesn't budge. "Because *you* didn't care enough to do it."

"I didn't know half the shit that went on that night, Rosey. You know that. Fuck, I didn't even know Ollie existed up until a few years ago when you just showed up right before floating back into the club like a fucking stain."

"If you didn't want me to stick around, you could have said."

"Right, cos you listen to everything I say," he snaps, arching a brow. "You know, I put up with so much fucking shit from you, Rosey, and you're still under my roof, living and breathing. You disrupt my club on a daily, you encourage the ol' ladies to go against my rules... shit, you even killed two members. You back chat, you piss off the Taylor's, you're never around to take care of Ollie the way you should." Those final words hurt the most. I take a few steps away from him, and he sighs. "We need to sleep on this and talk properly tomorrow. We're too angry to speak rationally right now."

I smirk. "Fuck you, Mav. You said it all perfectly."

Chapter Eleven

ROSEY

I tap lightly on the door. I don't know if I'm hoping she won't hear so I can walk away, or if all my energy is gone and I'm just too damn tired to make a noise. When Mum opens the door, she takes one look at me and opens it wider, allowing me to step inside.

Her flat isn't big. There's a small passage with a kitchen off to one side, a bedroom and bathroom to the other, and the living room at the end. It's clean and tidy, which surprises me seeing as she never used to care about things like that. I take a seat on the couch, and Mum pauses a television show she was watching. "Drink?" she asks, and

I nod. "I don't have anything with alcohol in," she admits. "The temptation is too much. But I have tea and coffee."

"Coffee," I mutter, and she disappears into the kitchen to make it.

I look around the room at the old-fashioned flower pictures on the wall. There's no photographs like in normal family homes. I doubt she even owns one picture of me as a kid. When she returns, she sits in an armchair and sips her own drink. "So, what's wrong?"

I shrug. "I had an argument with Maverick, and I have nowhere to go. I left my bank card at the clubhouse and I don't wanna go back there right now."

"Have you spoken to Ollie?"

"Yep. Tell me, how the hell did you bump into a kid you haven't seen in years?"

"I know a few of his friends. They said his name, and I just had an instinct. We got chatting and it confirmed my suspicions."

"What friends?" *I don't even know his friends.*

"Kids off the estate." She shrugs. "They're not bad kids really, they just need some love and stability."

I scoff. "Listen to you, mum of the year."

"If you've come for a fight, I'm in no mood, Rosey."

ALBERT

I shake my head. I'm in no place to argue right now either. "Can I take the couch? Just one night."

"Will you let me see Ollie again?"

I ponder her words before nodding. He wants to see her, and if I deny him, he'll make it a mission. "But we'll arrange it properly. No more street meets without me there."

I hear the front door banging and sit up. The room is dark, I must have fallen asleep before Mum left me to go to bed. Stretching, I hear Mum rushing to open the door.

"What the fuck, Con? I've been out here for five minutes," says a man's voice.

"Keep it down. I've got Rosey in there sleeping," she hisses back.

"I'm awake," I call out, checking my phone to see missed calls from Maverick and Albert. It's almost seven in the morning. Mum comes in and opens the curtains.

"Did you sleep well?" she asks.

"Yeah, actually." It surprises me after everything that happened yesterday.

A man appears in the doorway, and Mum smiles. "Rosey, this is Dougie." He nods, and I do the same.

"It's a little early for visitors," I say, wondering if she's still up to her old tricks, when men would call at her door at all hours of the day and night.

"I'm not a visitor," he says. "I live here."

I arch my brows and glance at Mum, who nods. "We've been together for a few months."

"I didn't realise." The way she limped into the café the other day explains it. She's always been with men who mistreat her, but I'm past worrying about my mum and her choice in men.

"We met when I returned here. I meant to tell you."

"It's fine. I should go and find Ollie," I say, standing.

"He's fine. He's with Ste," says Dougie, and I frown. *How does he know Ollie?* As if reading my mind, he adds, "Connie introduced us yesterday. He hangs around with my sister's kid. I just left hers. They stayed there last night."

"Right," I mutter. "Thanks." My mobile rings out, and I glance at Arthur's name. "I should take this," I say, heading for the door. I press it to my ear. "Yep?"

"You're driving my brother crazy, Red. What's the deal?"

"The deal is you killed my protégé and I'm upset about that."

I hear him snigger. "Business," he replies.

"How can I trust any of you now?" I ask. "You kept me out of it."

"Should I have hired you for the job, Red?" he muses. "What price would it have cost to bend your sudden morality?"

"I don't have time for this, Art. I've got to go and find my son."

"Come to the office, Rosey." He leaves no room for discussion as he disconnects the call. I growl in frustration. If I don't turn up there, he'll send someone to find me.

ALBERT

Arthur nods to the seat opposite his desk, and I lower into it. "Rosey's pissed, but she'll be okay," he tells me.

"You spoke to her?"

"I saw her," he tells me, and I clench my jaw. "She came to the office."

"Of her own free will?" He smirks. I bite down the words I want to spit about her being at his beck and call all the goddamn time. "Where was she last night?" Mav told me she'd left in a huff and refused to go back to the clubhouse.

"Bert, I don't pry into that shit. I told her straight why we had Archer removed. She understood and left. She's off the books," he throws in.

I sit up straighter. "What?"

"Is that a problem?"

"Yeah, she's good at her job. We need her."

"And she wants to step down. That was the whole reason Archer was here in the first place. Now you have Lauren. I don't see the problem." I sit in silence until he takes pity on me. "She's addictive," he starts. "I get it. But she's not gonna give you a happy ever after, Bert." I know he's right, but his words don't stop the ache I have in my chest.

"Maybe I don't want a conventional happy ever after. Maybe I like the fire she throws."

"It's like taming a wild cat, brother. Not worth it and too time-consuming."

"I seem to remember having this same conversation with you about Meli. Now, you're married and trying for a kid."

He nods, smiling. "Touché."

"I shouldn't have gone behind her back."

ALBERT

"It's business, Albert. If she can't keep the two separate, it definitely isn't going to work, fire or not." He sighs. "In other news, Tommy reckons the estate's gone quiet."

"That's good, isn't it?"

He shrugs. "Maybe. We've made enough noise to take the streets ourselves, but I feel like something's off. It's the calm before the storm."

"You worry too much. Call if you need me. I'm gonna find Red."

He laughs. "Like a fucking puppy dog."

I leave, not bothering to argue because, right now, I don't care what it looks like as long as she speaks to me.

I pull up at the MC and notice her car outside. I head in only for Mav to stop me, ordering me into his office. "She's looking for a place to move to," he tells me.

"Around here?" I ask.

Mav shrugs. "I wouldn't put it past her to move farther just to get away. She's upset. I've never seen her cry like that before, Albert. She cared for Archer." I know it's wrong, but jealousy surges through me. "We underestimated how much."

"She hasn't killed any of us, so that's a good sign."

He smirks. "Yet."

"I gotta level with you, Mav," I begin, sitting straighter. "I've had a group of kids from the estate followed. Ollie is hanging with some of the E15 boys." Archer managed to get that much intel before we took him out. The E15 boys were running the Abbey Road estate under Jenifer Hall's instruction before. We've since taken them over, and all the guys are saying the same—Ollie hangs out there, but he isn't involved or part of the gang. But that doesn't mean he isn't wanting to join them.

I relay all that to Mav, and he nods. "I'll take care of it."

"I was gonna tell Rosey," I add.

He shakes his head. "No. Wait until I've got more. I'll have his room turned over and speak to him."

I feel uneasy. "If Rosey finds out we knew this and didn't share it, she'll be pissed."

"She's already pissed. Besides, she's in denial, thinking the kid's just running through a bad patch."

"You don't think he is?" I ask.

"No. I had my suspicions but nothing concrete. Let me dig and then we'll tell her."

ALBERT

Rosey is packing her bags while Meli sits on her bed, pouting. When I appear, Meli leaves, gently squeezing my arm as she passes. "You going on holiday without me, Red?"

"I've lost my touch," she replies. "You're still walking around here breathing and shit. A few months ago, I'd have taken you all out."

I nod. "So, what happened?"

"I grew a conscience," she mutters, stuffing more clothes into the bag.

"You fell in love," I risk.

She scoffs. "Don't flatter yourself."

"That's why it hurts so much, Red. I lied and went behind your back, and I hurt you."

"Yeah, you did, and yes, it hurts, but don't think for one minute it's because I fell for you. I'm hurt you all got together and made this plan behind my back. I'm hurt you knew how much I wanted to help him yet you still had him taken out. And I'm hurt you brought Mav in on it, the only man I ever trusted."

I let her words take the hit on my chest. She's angry and lashing out, but it doesn't take the sting away. "We had to bring Mav in, he's a business associate."

"He's more than that to me, Albert," she yells. "At least, that's what I thought."

I trail my finger over her dressing table. "Where are you gonna go?"

She shrugs. "Away from this club. Away from you. I need a fresh start."

"It won't make the pain go away," I tell her. "Love doesn't just stop when you walk away."

"He had younger siblings," she mutters. "He helped to look after them. His mum needed the money he made to raise them."

"Red, you've killed enough people to know most had families. If we worried about that before every kill, there would be a hell of a lot more bad people in this world."

"I take down real bad people," she spits angrily. "Rapists, Paedophiles . . . not Archer. Not men just trying to help their families. Not men like you or Mav."

"Rapists and Paedophiles have families," I argue. "Someone cares about them."

"You know what I mean," she hisses. "They're hurting defenceless, vulnerable people."

"Archer wanted to kill me and Meli."

ALBERT

"In the beginning. He was just doing his job. But we gave him a better offer," she yells. "He was on our side. You know what I think, Albert?" She looks into my eyes. "I think you were jealous and that's why you did it."

I hang my head and place my hands on my hips. "It was business."

She moves closer. "So, you didn't care I was fucking him?"

I look up, narrowing my eyes. "You weren't."

"Maybe I was. I guess you'll never know."

Anger burns through me as I clench my fists. "Is that why you sobbed beside his dead body?" I snarl. She grins, shoving more clothes into her bag. I slam my fist into the drywall, and it shatters into pieces, falling to the floor. She arches a brow, unfazed by my outburst. "So, what we have—"

She laughs. It's cold, and her eyes are blazing with anger. "What we have?" she repeats. "Listen to yourself," she sneers. "We have nothing, Albert. It was sex. Just sex. People like us, we don't fall in love and live happily ever after. You're kidding yourself if that's what you thought would happen."

I take a minute to process her words, then I compose myself, pushing the anger away. I nod. "You're right." Her smile fades slightly. "I was getting carried away." I move to the door. "Arthur tells me you're stepping away?"

"I can't work with people I don't trust," she mutters.

"Makes sense," I say. "We have Lauren now, and she's got no kids to hold her back. Plus, she's more . . . manageable." I add a laugh. "Take care, Red." And I walk out, closing the door behind me as calm as I can.

ROSEY

I stare at the closed door. This is what I wanted, to walk away, so why does it twist my heart so much? I shake my head to clear the thoughts racing there. I have Ollie to think about, and I can't do that when Albert is taking up space in my head rent-free.

I finish packing and call Ollie. I'd left him a message already, telling him I have a plan, but this time, he picks up. "We're leaving the MC," I tell him.

"Where are we going?"

"I don't know. We'll find somewhere. A nice place where the air is fresher and it's less . . . busy."

"I don't wanna leave London," he snaps.

ALBERT

"Ollie, let's talk about it face to face."

"Fine. I'll meet you at Nan's place."

I roll my eyes. The kid's met her once, and now, she's his go-to. "Fine," I tell him, "I'm on my way."

Mum opens the door, and I follow her into the living room, where Ollie and a friend I've never met are sitting with Dougie, watching football. "Cuppa?" asks Mum, and I nod, following her back out and into the kitchen. "It's lovely having kids around the place," she tells me as she fills the kettle.

"Who's his friend?" I ask.

"Kyle."

"He looks older," I state.

She shrugs. "Maybe a year or so older. Dougie knows his dad."

"We've left the club," I tell her, and she pauses mid pouring hot water to look at me. "I think Ollie and I need a fresh start."

She places the kettle down and tuns to me. "Ollie is settled here. He's making friends."

"He'll make friends wherever we go."

"Is it because of Albert Taylor?" she asks.

I shake my head. "What makes you say that?"

"You came here with him that time and you've not mentioned him. I assumed you'd had a fall out."

"I have a lot of male friends, Mum. Doesn't mean I'm in any kind of relationship with them."

She goes back to the tea. "So, you and he weren't—"

"No," I snap. "What about Dougie? He seems settled here."

She hands me a cup of tea and smiles. "He's good for me. Don't get me wrong, we have our differences, but I like a bit of fire in the relationship."

I have flashbacks of when I was a child and she'd be screaming and fighting with bikers or whoever she was fucking that week. "I remember," I mutter dryly.

"Dougie rents out properties," she says thoughtfully. "Maybe you could stay in one until you figure out what you want."

"I know what I want, Mum. I want to leave here and start again. I only really came back to London to put some shit to bed. After I did that, I'd decided to stick around, but it was a mistake."

"Not really. It brought you back to me," she says.

I resist rolling my eyes. I never did understand how we'd fight like cat and dog one minute and just move forward like it never happened the next. "We can call or whatever."

Ollie comes in. "I'm not leaving here."

I scoff. "Sorry, who made you the person in charge?"

"I mean it. I'll just keep running away."

Mum smirks. "Who does he remind you of?"

"I ran away for very different reasons," I snap, glaring at her. "Not because I was having a tantrum. Ollie, there's nothing for us here."

"Apart from Nan," he points out. "And Mav, Hadley, and Meli."

"We can visit."

"I don't want to visit. I want to stay. I promise to be better at school."

I soften slightly. "Ollie, leaving isn't a punishment. I just think we need a fresh start."

"Because of Albert? Did he dump you?"

I frown, not realising he knew there was anything going on between me and Albert. "Look, I'm the adult and I'm telling you this is happening."

"You can't uproot my life because yours is messed up," he yells angrily. His words resonate with me. They're words I'd often say to my mum when she messed things up with another man. I swore I'd never be like her and here I am doing the same thing.

Dougie walks in. "Calm down," he tells Ollie, and Ollie hangs his head. My frown deepens. "Show some respect. Your mother knows what's best."

"Sorry," Ollie mutters.

"Ollie, go in the other room," I say, and he does without argument. I fix my glare on Dougie. "I don't need you to chastise my child."

He shrugs. "Apologies. I'm a youth worker and it's hard to break the habit. I have a way with troubled teens and—"

"He's not troubled," I cut in.

"Whatever you say," he mutters, holding up his hands.

"Yah know, maybe it would help to be closer to us," Mum says quietly. "Dougie is really good with the local kids. Ollie seems to respond well to him."

I scrub my face with my hands, feeling exhausted. "I have an empty place right upstairs," says Dougie. "Take it. I'll do you a good deal."

I sigh. "Is it furnished?" He nods. "Fine, but just until I decide what to do next."

ALBERT

Lauren is easy to work with. Way easier than Rosey. She's quick, clean, and doesn't mess around. She lures her victims, much the same as Rosey, but once she's got them where she wants them, she gets on with the job. I step outside and call for clean-up to remove the body. Lauren follows me out, gently running her hand down my back. "I could do with lunch, fancy joining me?"

I lock up the container so no one can wander in before clean-up arrives. "Sure. I know a place just around the corner."

I take her to a small deli. I know the owner, and when he sees me, he smiles wide, showing us to his best table. "Will you always hang around when I do work for you?" Lauren asks while the waiter pours us some water.

"No," I tell her. "I just happened to be in the area. How the hell did you get him there?" I ask, impressed she'd managed to meet the target, befriend him, and get him to the container at the docks, all within a few hours.

"I played the damsel in distress, needing a strong man to help me collect some belongings from a shipment container for my new flat." She pops an olive into her mouth. "Admit it, you're impressed."

I laugh. "Actually, I am. It was quick and clean and away from prying eyes. Arthur will be happy."

The door opens and I happen to glance up right as Rosey enters, followed by her mum. She doesn't see me right away, not until the waiter leads her past our table to seat her just to the left of us. As she sits, she catches my eye but recovers quickly, smiling at something her mum says.

"Well, this is awkward," Lauren murmurs.

I shrug. "Not really," I lie, because every cell in my body wants to go to her. "Where were we?"

"You were about to tell me how amazing I am and how you'd like me to go to dinner with you."

I grin and ask, "Isn't that what this is?"

She runs her painted fingernail over the back of my hand. "Maybe we could double date with your brother?"

"Arthur?" I laugh again. "He doesn't double date. He doesn't date. Meli would be suspicious if he suddenly took her to dinner."

ALBERT

She bites her lower lip. "I think it would be good to get to know one another. It's how I like to work."

I catch Rosey's eye again and force a smile at Lauren. "Fine, I'll see what I can do."

Chapter Twelve

ROSEY

I've been in the new flat for a week, but I've done nothing to it because I don't want Ollie to get too settled here. My plan is to move away once he gets my mum out his system, which I'm sure he will soon enough. But right now, he's settled and happy. He's got a lot of friends who come and go with him, and I realise now just how restricting the clubhouse was for him. Maverick didn't like strangers in and out of the place, so Ollie would never bring anyone back. And surprisingly, Mum's been a constant this week, popping in every day to see how I am. It's almost like we're living a normal life.

ALBERT

But as I sit opposite Albert's table, where he smiles and laughs with the woman who replaced me, I feel that familiar heartache. I find myself zoning out of my mum's gossip about some of the women in our block of flats and trying to listen in to what Albert is talking about. He looks animated, and his eyes sparkle with affection. I try to remember a time when he looked at me like that—there isn't one. Most of the time, I annoyed him. They eat, chatting the entire time, and then Albert gets the bill and stands, placing his hand at the small of Lauren's back before guiding her out. He didn't bother to look back. It's almost like we're strangers. "You could just go and speak to him," Mum says, cutting into my haze.

"Huh?"

"Albert. You could just chase him down and speak to him."

I laugh. "Please, that ship has sailed."

"Has it?" She looks amused. "You spent the last twenty minutes staring at him."

"I did not," I mutter and check my watch. "I have to shoot. I've got to meet Meli."

She narrows her eyes. "I thought you were done with the club?"

"I am, but Meli's different. She's like my sister."

Meli looks delighted to see me. She slides a brightly coloured cocktail in my direction as I sit down. "You look good," she tells me.

"Liar," I mutter. "I look tired and worn out."

She smiles sympathetically. "How's things?"

I shrug. "Good . . . different, I guess."

"You don't sound so sure."

I sigh heavily. "Mum thinks I'm depressed. She offered me some tablets she used to take."

"Depressed?" Meli repeats. "What makes her think that?"

"I feel exhausted all the time. Everything seems so much effort lately. Mum's been great. She pops in every day to check on me and she's been handling stuff at the school with Ollie."

Meli looks concerned. "Have you spoken to a doctor?"

I shake my head. "No. You know I hate doctors. I don't want to waste their time."

ALBERT

"If you think you're depressed, it's not wasting their time. The last time I checked, your mum wasn't qualified to make those diagnoses."

"She's just trying to help. Since Archer, things have been harder," I admit. "Everything seems so out of control."

"You know you can speak to me anytime," she offers. "Just because you left the club doesn't mean you can't come over to the house to see me."

I nod. "I just don't want to bump into Albert."

"He's a big boy, he'll get over it."

"Is he? Over it, I mean?" I ask, picking at invisible fluff on my jumper.

She smirks. "Are you missing him?"

I scowl. "Forget I asked."

"You know what he's like, Rosey. He won't show me if he's upset or hurting." Her mobile rings and she glances at it. "Hold on a sec, let me take this or he'll track me down," she says, pressing it to her ear. "Arthur, what could you possibly need? I saw you twenty minutes ago." She goes silent, listening to him. "Really? You know I can't cook." She nods even though he can't see her. "Fine." And then she hangs up. "Speak of the devil. Albert invited himself over for dinner this evening. Arthur's getting someone in to cook, thank God."

"That's a lot of effort just for Albert."

"Oh, he's not coming alone. It's a business thing." She shrugs.

"Lauren?" I ask.

She winces. "Yeah. Apparently, she wants to get to know them better." She places her hand over mine. "You could always come along."

"Don't be ridiculous."

"We both know you miss him, Rosey. Turn up and pretend you didn't know he was coming."

I ponder her words. "I am mad he ignored me earlier," I admit.

She grins. "Is that the old Rosey I see? I don't think you're depressed at all. I think you just need to have some good old-fashioned Rosey fun."

ALBERT

Lauren is way too familiar for my liking. We share a past, but that's exactly what it is, the past. Arthur pours me a drink, and I take it gratefully. "I had to get a chef in," he tells us with a laugh. "Meli isn't the cooking type."

ALBERT

Meli scowls. "I prefer warning."

"My fault," I say, holding up a hand. "Apologies. Although we could have just gotten a takeout."

"Lauren, have you known Albert long?" Meli asks.

"Long enough to have known what he was like before the suits and unapologetic attitude," she says with a fond smile.

"Oh, shit, did you two . . ." she trails off. "Does Rosey know?"

I frown. "There's nothing between me and Rosey."

"Leave it, Meli," Arthur warns.

"There was clearly something," Lauren continues. "She didn't take her eyes off you earlier."

"Do we need to discuss Rosey right now?" I ask, arching a brow and glancing between the two women.

"Let's go through to the dining room," Arthur suggests, changing the subject.

We sit down, and the chef brings out the first course. I open the wine right as the front door opens and we hear Rosey shout out for Meli. Meli cringes. "In here," she answers.

"What is she doing here?" Arthur hisses.

Meli shrugs. "You know she likes to come around a lot."

"We haven't seen her all week, why would she turn up now?"

Rosey steps into the dining room, smiling wide. "Did you forget my invite, Art?" I take in her short dress and heels. She knew I'd be here—it's my favourite outfit.

Arthur narrows his eyes. "It's a private dinner party."

"Arthur," hisses Meli, "don't be rude."

Rosey sits the other side of me, and I immediately sit straighter. Her perfume fills my nostrils, and I wipe my hands down my trousers. Knowing how unpredictable she can be makes me nervous. "It's fine. We're all friends here, right, Bert?" She grabs a napkin and lays it on her lap. "Although you were rather rude earlier when you didn't speak to me."

"Isn't that what you wanted?" I mutter.

She grabs my fork and stabs at my prawn starter. "Are you still moody because of what I said?"

"Nope," I say on a sigh.

"Because I know it was harsh, but I thought we were on the same page. I didn't realise you wanted a relationship. It took me by surprise." She's trying to embarrass me by telling the table our conversation, and I don't appreciate it.

ALBERT

She continues to eat some of my prawns, closing her eyes in appreciation. "Oh my god, these are amazing."

"Do we have to do this now?" asks Arthur, throwing down his napkin and glaring at her.

"Let her get it out her system," I say, folding my arms over my chest and staring straight ahead. "She won't stop until she has."

"And what, a week later, you're having dinner with Lauren," Rosey continues, smiling in Lauren's direction. "A nice family get-together." Lauren tips her wine glass slightly, like she's raising a toast to family. She smirks and takes a sip, and I'm reminded that I'm sitting between two deadly women.

"Does that bother you?" I ask. "Because from what I hear, you've got your family around you these days."

"Are you keeping tabs on me, Bert?" asks Rosey, grinning playfully.

"What do you want, Rosey? Why are you here?"

"To see Meli," she says simply, with a shrug of her shoulders.

"She's entertaining guests," snaps Arthur. "Or can't you read the room?"

Rosey winces. "It's my ADHD. I don't tend to take a hint."

Meli stands suddenly. "Look, she can stay for dinner, it's not a problem. I'll let the chef know." And she disappears into the kitchen.

"Seriously, Rosey," Arthur growls, "I don't need the hassle."

"It's just dinner, Art. Relax," she replies, winking.

Rosey takes my wine, draining the glass. "So, how's business?"

"You don't need to know," snaps Arthur.

"Ouch. Rude."

"What about you?" Lauren asks, leaning around me to see Rosey. "Are you getting much work?"

"I'm taking a career break."

"Not the sort of business to do that, is it? Before you know it, everyone will forget who you are. You'll be replaced," says Lauren. "Again."

"I'm not worried."

Lauren places her hand on my thigh, and Rosey catches the move. I don't remove it purely out of anger. I want her to hurt, like her words hurt me.

Meli returns. "Sorted."

ALBERT

Rosey tops up my glass of wine but keeps hold of it. "I always hate these things," she says to no one in particular. "They were invented for couples," she continues. "It's always 'bring a plus one'."

"Well, you weren't invited, Red," Arthur reminds her.

"I couldn't have brought a plus one anyway," she says with a laugh. "You killed him . . . remember?" I roll my eyes. It's going to be a long night.

Dinner is brought in and, for a while, the conversation dies down. Rosey being here is making things awkward, which I'm certain was her intention.

We're almost through dessert when Lauren returns to the earlier conversation of our past. "Meli, I didn't finish telling you about Albert and me," she says, and I inwardly groan. "We met when I was sixteen. I was working in the fish and chip shop on Barrell Street. It's a vaping shop these days. He used to come in every Friday night to get two large bags of chips for him and his brothers to share." She smiles fondly, placing her hand over my own.

"He was always polite. Then, one day, he came in when I was getting hassle off an ex, remember?" she asks me, and I nod. "Albert threw him out on his arse, and I was in awe. I didn't know he had it in him." She laughs, laying her head on my shoulder, and I marvel at how different she is compared to Rosey, who would never show affection towards me, especially not in public. "I fell head over heels."

I glance at her. "Did you?" I ask, smirking, because that's news to me.

She nods, grinning wide. "I wasn't about to tell you and give you a big head."

"Funny," says Rosey, leaning forward to look Lauren in the eye. "When I asked him who you were, he said he hardly knew you."

Lauren's smirk doesn't fade. In fact, it gets bigger as she too leans forward. "I always worried if my man played down knowing another woman. Secrets are like cancer in a relationship."

"He also said there was nothing between you. Did he forget to tell you that?" asks Rosey. "Because the way you keep pawing at him like a possessed freak tells me you're not on the same page."

"We're getting reacquainted, getting to know one another again," Lauren quips. "I have no doubt where it'll lead."

My patience is out and I stand abruptly, causing both women to stare up at me. "Word, now," I say, dropping

ALBERT

my napkin on the table. "Rosey," I clarify and head for Arthur's office. For once, she follows without me having to make a fuss. She closes the door, and I spin to face her. "What the fuck?"

She smiles innocently. "I'm being polite."

"You're getting to know your next victim. I see it, and she can see it. Don't take me for an idiot."

She covers her chest innocently. "Albert, why would I want to kill your girlfriend?"

"Firstly, she isn't my girlfriend. Secondly, she replaced you because you wanted out. Unless you're having second thoughts, I suggest you back the fuck off."

She moves closer, and I recognise the heated look in her eyes. I watch her hand cautiously as it reaches out, resting gently on my chest. "Don't be mad with me, Bert." Her false niceness just annoys me more.

"You should go," I say, stepping around her, "and let me enjoy dinner in peace." I head for the door, and as I reach for the handle, she mutters something I don't quite hear. I turn back to her. "I don't know what you want from me, Rosey?" I snap. "You blow hot and cold and I'm fucking exhausted by it. You wanted out, you're out. You wanted to walk away from me, I'm letting you. Go and do whatever the fuck it is you do now you've left me and the club. But stop showing up in my life and giving me mixed signals because I'm tired of it, and honestly," I look her up and down, "I'm tired of you." I leave the room, slamming the door hard. As I re-join the dinner, I hear the front door open and close, and I breathe a sigh of relief.

"All sorted?" asks Arthur.

I nod, ignoring the daggers Meli is sending my way. "She seemed pleasant," Lauren jokes. "Will she be around much?"

"She doesn't work for us anymore, if that's what you're asking," I mutter, topping up my wine.

"But she's very much a part of all our lives," Meli adds.

"Your life," I correct.

"I'm worried about her," Meli blurts out, and as much as I try to ignore it, I can't.

"Why?" I ask.

"She mentioned her mum wants to give her anti-depressants."

"Sounds like a damn good idea to me," says Arthur. "She's been up and down like a crazy bitch these past months. She's unpredictable and makes rash decisions. Maybe they'll help stabilise her moods."

ALBERT

Meli glares at him. "If she's depressed, she should see a doctor, not take her mum's pills. Her mum hasn't been around, but suddenly, she's an expert on Rosey? I'm worried."

"She's a grown-up, Meli. She can take care of herself," Arthur reassures her.

Meli looks across the table to me, and I shrug. "He's right, she's an adult."

"Do you think she's depressed?" she asks.

I shake my head. "But she's been acting weird lately. Something's changed. She's making huge changes in her life with no real explanation."

"You killed her friend," Meli reminds me. "I don't think she's ever lost anyone close to her and it shook her up. Maybe it reminded her how precious life is."

"She's a trained killer, she can't grow a conscience," Arthur jokes. "It's why we had to get rid of her."

"She's not a robot," Meli yells. "Will you get rid of me when I become of no use to you?" Arthur rolls his eyes, which only infuriates his wife more. She stands, scraping back her chair. "Maybe you should sleep in one of the spare rooms for a few nights," she hisses, and his eyes widen. "I don't feel like being very useful right now." She stomps off.

He turns his anger to me. "I knew it would end like this," he snaps. "And somehow, I'm in trouble. Why didn't you just stay the hell away from the psychotic bitch?" He storms off too, and I'm left with Lauren, who looks amused by the whole thing.

"I'll take you home," I mutter.

ROSEY

I laugh at Meli's dramatics. The fact she's ringing me from her master bedroom while I'm curled up on a second-hand sofa tells me she isn't as hard done to as she likes to make out. "Don't halt the baby-making because of me," I tell her. "I'm fine."

She sighs heavily. "What happened with you and Albert?"

"He did what they all do, Meli. He walked away." The line goes silent for a second, so I add, "It's fine, though. I expected it. It's kind of my own fault."

"Don't say that," she murmurs.

ALBERT

"It's true, isn't it? It's the same old story. I did everything I could to push him away until he got tired of fighting me. I got what I wanted."

"But it's not what you wanted at all, is it? You love him, Rosey. I wish you'd just be honest."

I lay my head back and look up at the ceiling. "Why did he have to kill Archer?" I ask, my heart twisting painfully. "Everything was going good until then."

"Did you book in with a doctor?" she asks, changing the subject. I eye the pack of pills mum gave me.

"No, I'll be fine."

"You keep saying that, but who are you trying to convince?"

I take the packet and pop out a small white pill, turning it over in my palm. It looks harmless enough. Maybe it'll help. Maybe taking this pill will stop the hurt, lost feeling that's ripping me apart. I stick it in my mouth and grab the glass of water from the table. "Do me a favour, make things right with Arthur," I tell her. "I'll call you later in the week."

I wake with a pounding headache. Ollie is watching me from the opposite chair. "Are you okay?" he asks.

I frown, stretching out my aching muscles. "I must have fallen asleep on here," I say, pushing to sit up.

"I tried to wake you this morning," he tells me. "You were dead to the world."

I snatch my phone off the table and gasp aloud when the clock reads four in the afternoon. "Jesus, I slept all night and most of the day?"

"I got in from school and you were still out of it," he continues. I glance at the packet of pills guiltily, they're clearly stronger than I thought. "Anyway, I gotta go." He stands. "Dougie's taking me for a drive in his Subaru. I hope the lads from school see me in it." He grins, heading out.

Ten minutes pass before Mum arrives, letting herself in. "Hey," she says brightly, freezing when she spots me still on the couch. "Oh dear, everything okay?"

I nod. "I think so. I took one of your pills. What did you say they were again? There's no name on the box."

She shrugs. "Dougie gets them. They're good, though, right?"

"Not really. I passed out for almost eighteen hours."

ALBERT

She smiles. "You must have needed the rest. Stick with them, they'll soon have you feeling right."

"Do you still take them?" I ask.

She nods. "Dougie says they help. I'm less of a cow when I'm on them." She adds a laugh, but I'm not convinced. "Speaking of him, he's out for most of the evening. Fancy coming over to watch a film?"

I nod. "Sure. Let me shower and change."

We order takeout and watch two movies. I check my watch and it's almost nine in the evening. "Ollie isn't back," I state.

"He's with Dougie, he'll be fine. They're getting along so well. Take a pill, and I'll text them to see when they'll be home."

"I'm fine, I don't like how they knocked me out," I say.

She takes the pack and hands me one anyway. "Trust me, they'll soon begin their magic."

I need magic right now, so I take it.

Chapter Thirteen

ALBERT

I tap my thumb against the steering wheel, slowing down as a group of youths cross the road. As I pull off, I notice one of the kids making an exchange with a passing guy on a pushbike. I frown, pulling over a little farther down and glancing in my mirror. It's Ollie. I check my watch. It's noon, and he should be in school.

I get out the car and lean against it. "Ollie," I shout, and he glances back. "Over here." He makes his way towards me. "Why aren't you in school?"

"What's it gotta do with you?" he asks, smirking.

"Everything. Does your mum know you're bunking off?"

ALBERT

He shrugs. "Mum's happy, that's all you need to know."

"What the fuck's that supposed to mean?"

He grins, glancing over at a Subaru as it slows to a stop. The windows are blacked out, so I can't make out who's inside, but Ollie heads off and gets in the back. It pulls away at speed, the tyres screeching.

I get back in my car and put a call in on the handsfree to Maverick. "To what do I owe the pleasure?" he drawls when he picks up.

"You heard from Rosey recently?"

"Nope. She ain't answering my calls. Meli tried too, no luck there either. She's made herself clear. I can't keep chasing her."

"I just bumped into Ollie. He's skipping school."

Maverick laughs. "We all did that at one time or another."

"She walked away from us all to concentrate on him. I know she'd make him stay in school."

Mav sighs. "You're right. I'll send someone to her place. Unless you wanna go?"

"Not a good idea. I saw her two weeks ago and told her I was done with her."

"How did she take it?"

"I don't know. I mean, I'm not dead yet, so better than I expected." I stop outside Lauren's house. She's sitting on the front step and smiles wide when she sees me. "I gotta shoot. Let me know how you get on."

I step out the car. "You waiting for me?"

She bites her lower lip seductively, and I try not to roll my eyes. She's been trying everything to get me to fall for her. Grabbing my hand, she leads me inside. The place is bustling with people. I frown and ask, "What's this?"

"A housewarming," she says with a shrug.

"Lauren, I don't need a roomful of people seeing us together," I snap.

"We're old friends, it's not suspicious. Come and see my brother. It's been ages." I let her pull me towards a group of people. I recognise Dax the second he turns to face me. He grins wide, holding out his hand, which I shake.

"Well, if it isn't the legend, Albert Taylor," he greets. "Good to see you, man."

"Dax, it's been a while." He grabs a bottle of beer from a nearby bucket and passes it to me.

"I've heard you're doing good for yourself," he tells me, and Lauren hooks her arm through mine, resting her head on my shoulder. "I'm pleased for you, Albert. And you're looking fantastic. Money suits you."

I drank way more than I'd planned to, and as I flop down on Lauren's couch, I pull out my mobile to see some missed calls. Before I get a chance to check them, Lauren climbs onto my lap, facing me. "What a great night," she says, taking my bottle of beer and sipping some. "Admit it, you had fun."

I smile. It was good to catch up with her brother. "I need to call a cab," I tell her.

"Or . . ." She grins. "You could stay here?"

"That's not a good idea."

She groans. "Just give in to yourself," she says. "I know you feel it too. Why won't you let yourself go?" She places the bottle on the table, practically pushing her breasts into my face. Then she runs her hands over my cheeks. "We have something," she whispers.

"Lauren, I—"

She cuts me off by pressing her mouth to mine. I don't react, even though I saw it coming. She rocks herself against me, thrusting her tongue in my mouth desperately, and I should be feeling something. Lord knows she's hot as sin, but all I can think about is Rosey. Lauren pulls back, eyeing me with annoyance. "Seriously, Albert, give me something here."

I take her by the waist and lift her from me. "I'm sorry, but I'm in love with someone else and leading you on would be a shit thing to do. So, I'm gonna go, and we'll pretend this didn't happen."

I step outside and open my phone. Maverick's called me three times, so I return his call first. "About time," he snaps. "You send me to check on Rosey and then don't pick up my calls?"

"Apologies, I was . . . never mind. Is she okay?"

"Not really. First of all, her mum was there acting cagey. She really didn't want to let us in. Anyway, eventually, she did, and Rosey was asleep. So deep in a sleep, I couldn't wake her at all."

"What does that mean, Mav?" I snap impatiently.

"When she did eventually stir, she was groggy and disorientated. I'm back at the clubhouse swapping my bike for a car so I can get her out of there."

"You think she's in danger?"

"I think she's off her face on drugs, Albert. And there's no way she took that shit voluntarily."

"Come get me on the way. I'll send you my location."

As we approach Rosey's door, it opens and a man steps out, fastening his jeans. I exchange a wary look with Mav, and as we come to a stop, we block his exit. "Can I help you?" he asks, irritated by our presence.

"We're looking for Rosey," says Mav.

He smirks. "She's asleep."

I focus on where his stubby fingers are fastening his belt and anger pulsates wildly in my veins. "Explain why the hell you're leaving her place at this hour, fastening your jeans."

He almost laughs. "She's my fucking stepdaughter, ain't no funny business going on. Maybe you should tell me why the hell you're turning up here at this hour."

"She never mentioned a stepdad to us," says Mav.

"Yeah, well, she didn't mention no boyfriend to me," he replies.

There's a stumbling from inside and we all turn as Rosey hobbles into the hall. "What the hell's going on?" she hisses, looking like she's just woken. Her eyes fall to me. "What are you doing here?"

"I came to check on you," I tell her, concern replacing the anger. She looks exhausted and confused. I step closer, cupping her cheek with my hand to get a close look at her pupils, but she steps back, lowering her eyes to the ground.

"I'm fine. I don't need you checking up on me."

"What have you taken?" I ask.

"You heard her, she doesn't want you here," the guy snaps.

"I don't even know who the fuck you are," I say, "and I'm assuming you have no idea who the hell I am, but it would be a mistake to assume I'm not important, so run along and go about your business."

"No, Dougie, stay," says Rosey, reaching for him and tugging him inside. "You need to leave, Albert. And don't come back here." She closes the door in our faces.

"Dougie," Mav repeats. "You think that's Dougie Harrison?"

I nod. "How many idiots called Dougie could there be around here?"

ALBERT

"Shit, we gotta get Rosey and Ollie out of here," he mutters.

"Looking at the state of her, she's not going to come willingly."

ROSEY

"Where's Ollie?" I mumble, taking a seat on the couch. I grip my forehead, trying to slow the dizziness that I get whenever I stand. "What time is it?"

"Time for your next pill," mutters Dougie, holding out his hand.

I shake my head and instantly feel sick. "No, they're not helping."

"Me and your mum are taking care of Ollie. You need to rest to recover from whatever virus this is," he tells me. I've been suffering for two weeks with sickness, dizzy spells, and hot sweats. I'm so weak, I struggle to stand.

"Maybe I need to see the doctor," I mumble, closing my eyes and resting my head back.

"Or maybe you need to be a good girl and take your medication," he replies, pressing his thumb to my chin and tugging it until my mouth falls open. He places the pill on my tongue, then holds a bottle of water to my mouth. I swallow, and he brushes his thumb over my wet lips. "See, it wasn't so hard." I can't respond, and my eyes are heavy. I feel myself being lifted and carried. "Let's go somewhere more comfortable," he whispers.

"Dougie, I'm worried you've given her too high a dose." It's my mum's voice I hear, but she sounds muffled and far away.

"Connie, I don't need your advice," says Dougie. "We do this my way, understand?"

"What are we going to do about the biker?"

"He got the message. Rosey told them to leave her alone. We don't have to do a damn thing, baby."

"Them?" Mum repeats. "He came back with others?"

"He came back with Albert Taylor. He stood there lording over me like I was scum." Dougie laughs. "If only he knew the power I have."

"Albert saw Rosey?" Mum sounds anxious.

"Relax, Con. Rosey told him to stay away. He's gone."

"I don't know, Dougie. He doesn't seem the kind to just walk away. That biker must have told him what a mess she was."

"That wouldn't have happened if you'd done your job and kept him out yesterday."

"I didn't have much choice. He shoved his way in here," Mum snaps, and I hear the sound of a slap. She cries out, and I'm transported back to when I was a small child and I'd cower away while she took a beating from whichever guy she was dating that month.

"Don't fucking use that tone with me, Connie, or I swear I'll have you both on that bed being fucked." His words startle me, and my breathing quickens. What the hell does he mean by that? I feel a finger in my mouth, and I instantly gag. "It's not time for you to wake just yet, gorgeous. We have plans," comes Dougie's voice. There's a pill on my tongue and then water. I have no choice but to swallow as he holds my mouth closed. I feel a sheet being removed from my body, which means I'm naked. My heart slams hard in my chest, then my mind goes fuzzy again, and I inwardly scream as I disappear into the darkness.

I squint as light hits my eyes. *Why is it so bright?* "Thank God," whispers Meli as she comes into view. "I thought you were gonna sleep forever."

I frown in confusion. *How did I get here?* "Ollie?" My throat is dry, and my voice doesn't sound like my own as I croak the word out.

"He's downstairs. Mav's dealing with him."

I try to sit up, but my arms don't feel like my own. They're heavy and shaky. "Mum?" I ask, giving up and laying still.

"You look like crap. I bet you're hungry too," Meli says. "How about I get Mama B to make you something good? You've lost a tonne of weight."

"Meli?" I murmur, and she lowers her eyes.

"Albert's coming back. He'll tell you everything then." She leaves before I can protest, and I stare at the closed door, wondering what the hell's happened and how I ended up back in my old bedroom at the clubhouse.

ALBERT

I pace the office. "How the fuck do I tell her?"

Maverick scrubs his hands over his face and groans loudly. "She's gonna kill them."

ALBERT

"Good, that's a thought I can live with."

Meli pops her head in. "Great, you're back. She's awake."

Dread fills my stomach. "How's Ollie?" I ask.

Mav groans again. "He's not happy he's here, put it that way."

"Let me talk to him first. Then I'll see Rosey."

I find Ollie playing darts on his own. I take a seat at a table and watch in silence until he reluctantly acknowledges me. "Why am I here, and why can't I see Mum?"

"When did you last see her?"

He shrugs. "A week ago. She's been ill, so I stayed at Nan's to give her a break."

"And Dougie, was he there?"

"Yeah. Why?"

"You remember the last time I saw you, Ollie?" I ask, and he pales slightly. "Why weren't you at school?"

"I just wanna see my mum and then I wanna go back to Nan's place," he snaps.

I groan, rubbing my forehead. "What have you gotten yourself into, Ollie?"

"Nothing," he yells, and I arch a brow at his sudden overreaction. I see some of the other bikers look over, but

Mav's there to keep them calm. I stand abruptly and push my face into his.

"You wanna be big and tough, kid? You think you're ready for that?" I hiss. "Cos I can arrange that for you. I know plenty of bad people, way worse than Dougie fucking Harrison."

He leans far back to get away from me, his eyes wide with fear. "If I don't go back . . ." he trails off and lowers his eyes to the ground.

"He'll do what? Cos I'd love him to turn up here and try anything."

"You don't get it," he mutters. "I owe him."

"Owe him what?" He keeps quiet. "Money?" He shakes his head. "Drugs?" He glances up but doesn't deny it. "You're taking drugs?"

"No. It wasn't my fault," he cries. "But he said it was, and now I owe him, or he'll hurt Nan and Mum."

Mav heads over, looking concerned. "Why didn't you say something?"

"Because he told me what he'd do to them if I did," he mumbles.

"Newsflash, Ollie, Dougie ain't shit around here. I am. He won't get near your mum," snaps Mav.

"And Nan?" he asks.

Mav looks at me. "She wouldn't come with us, Ollie," I admit. "We tried."

There's a real fear in Ollie's expression. His eyes widen and his mouth opens and closes a few times before he makes a run for the door. Mav intercepts, grabbing him around the waist and hauling him into a seat. "Not so fast, kid. We're gonna sort this. Trust us."

"He'll hurt her," he cries.

"I've known your nan a long time, Ollie, and she can look after herself," Mav says.

I place a hand on Ollie's shoulder. "We'll bring you in on it," I tell him, and Mav glares at me. "He needs to know what's going on," I say to Mav, "or he'll try and save her by himself. He's stubborn like his mother." I turn back to Ollie. "You wanna run with the real men? Cos those shitheads, aren't men, Ollie. They just think they are. Let's go and see your mum, and then we'll go to church," I say.

"Jesus, you want my patch too?" snaps Mav, and I slap him on the back with a laugh.

"Nah, it suits you better."

ROSEY

I'm sitting up in bed, and for the first time in weeks, my vision is beginning to clear. The foggy feeling I've suffered is lifting, and I finally feel like this virus is coming to an end. The door opens and Ollie rushes in, followed by Albert. He stops by the edge of my bed and eyes me warily. "You look terrible," he tells me.

I grin. "Thanks. I actually feel like I'm getting better."

"You've been sick for weeks," Ollie tells me.

"Has Nan been looking after you?" I try hard to remember for myself, but everything seems so hazy. He nods. "Where is she?" Ollie looks back over his shoulder to Albert, and I'm immediately suspicious. "Why am I here?"

Albert squeezes Ollie's shoulder gently. "You wanna stick around or go back to Mav?" he asks.

Ollie heads for the door. "I'll see you in church?" he asks, and Albert nods.

Once he's gone, Albert sits on the bed. "How are you feeling?"

"What the hell is going on?"

"You've been MIA for just over two weeks, Rosey," he says.

I laugh. "I've been at home fighting a virus."

ALBERT

"A virus . . . or these?" he asks, pulling my pill packet from his pocket. "I found them on your table beside your bed."

"I've been a little down," I admit. "They were to help."

"They were keeping you asleep, keeping you laid up in bed."

I frown. "Don't be ridiculous."

"There's something else I need to tell you," he adds.

Maverick bursts in, taking me by surprise. "We got a big problem," he says. "The police are here . . . for Ollie."

I throw the sheets back. "No," snaps Albert. "You should stay here. You don't know everything yet."

"He's my son," I growl, pushing to stand on weak legs. I grab his arm for support, and he reluctantly helps me to walk.

Downstairs, the police are talking to Ollie, and Mum is by the door with Dougie. "What's going on?" I ask Mum. She looks away, but I don't miss the guilt on her face. A female police officer ushers me away from Mum, and Albert follows.

"Ollie is under their care, he can't stay here," she gently tells me. I'm confused, and my expression must show it, because she goes on to add, "An emergency care order was granted last week."

I think my heart stutters a few times before her words process in my brain. Albert takes my hand to steady me as I sway. Lack of food and the shock of her words are making me faint. "What the hell are you talking about?" Albert demands.

The officer unfolds a piece of paper and holds it for us to see. I scan my eyes over it. "I don't understand," I whisper.

"Your mother and stepfather were granted a temporary care order as an emergency. A social worker called to see you several times leading up to this, but you were always . . . well, you weren't really with it."

"Of course, I wasn't, I've been ill," I argue. "Mum," I say, glaring across the room at her for confirmation. She remains silent. "I swear, I had a virus of some kind and I've not been well. But I'm much better now," I explain desperately.

The officer shrugs. "There's nothing I can do, I'm afraid. A social worker will be in contact to explain everything. There will be steps you need to complete before the next hearing."

"When will that be?" I cry.

ALBERT

"I'm not sure. Like I said, the social worker will have all the details."

The officers sitting with Ollie stand. He searches the room until his eyes land on me and guilt hits me hard. He's pleading with his eyes for me to stop this as they lead him away. "Do something," I yell, glaring at Maverick. "He's your half-brother, can't you take him?"

Mav shakes his head. "I tried that, but they're not interested. We have to let him go."

"No," I cry, rushing towards them. Albert wraps an arm around my waist, and I fight against him, screaming as Ollie is lead away. Mum looks back one last time before following, and I crumble in Albert's arms, sobs shaking my body.

Chapter Fourteen

ALBERT

I've never seen Rosey like this. She's always so strong and composed, but right now, as she buries her face into her hands, sobbing so hard she wretches, I see how vulnerable she is. I sit on the floor behind her, wrapping my arms around her weak body and whispering words of comfort. "I've got the number for Ollie's social worker here," Mav says. "We'll call and ask them to explain."

"What's the point? He's already gone," Rosey sobs.

Meli and Hadley crouch in front of her, each taking one of Rosey's hands. "Get up off the floor, Rosey," Meli says firmly. "You can't fight battles from down here." They tug her to stand, and I follow. "We need a plan, but first, you need to eat and get cleaned up." They lead her away from me.

"Let's call this social worker," Mav says, slapping me on the shoulder. "Find out what the fuck we're dealing with."

We go to his office, and he calls the number. When she answers, he explains he's Ollie's half-brother, but she insists on coming to see Rosey tomorrow rather than talk over the telephone, much to Mav's annoyance.

Mav then calls church, but I'm in no mood to go over the shit load of crap we know so far, so I head up in search of Rosey.

Hadley is on the bed, and Meli is blow drying Rosey's wet hair. I take the hairdryer from Meli, and the twins slip out of the room. Running my fingers through her hair, I continue what Meli started. After a few minutes, she turns to face me, taking it from me and turning it off. "Tell me everything."

I sit on the bed. "I spotted Ollie skipping school a couple weeks ago and passed it to Mav. He went to see you and found you out of it. He wanted to get you to the clubhouse, so we came back for you, only you told us to leave." She frowns. "Don't you remember?" She shakes her head. "We watched your place until Dougie left and we came back for you, Red. You were naked, and you didn't even stir when we carried you out of there."

"The pills are anti-depressants," she says.

"No, they're sleeping tablets. So strong, Doc says they're enough to put you out for twelve hours straight. They're not even prescribed in this country. They're foreign, and we're not convinced they're for human consumption."

"Mum said . . ." She shakes her head, still looking confused. "I just wanted to forget," she adds in a whisper.

I stroke a thumb down her cheek, cupping her jaw. "Archer?"

She shakes her head and mumbles, "You."

I close my eyes briefly as her words cut me. "Did you eat?"

"What happened to me?" she asks. "When I was out of it?"

I take her hand and pull her to stand. "Doc reckons that shit won't be fully out your system for a few days. Rest." I lead her to the bed and pull the sheets back.

"Albert, I need to know if anything happened."

I shrug. "I don't know, Red. You'll need Doc to exam you."

"Get him here now. I need to know."

ALBERT

Doc arrives within minutes, telling me he was already on his way to see how Rosey was doing. I show him to the room, and I'm about to leave when she takes my hand. "Please, stay."

Doc glances up from his bag. "It's quite personal, Rosey. Maybe he should wait outside."

"I want him here," she says firmly, and I nod. I won't leave her when she's asking me to stay, so I pull up a chair while she removes her bottoms and climbs into bed. Doc places a sheet over her stomach to her parted knees, and I take her hand again. "Ollie didn't want to go with them," she whispers, her eyes full of pain.

"I know," I say. "We'll get him back."

"Why would they take him from me?" she asks. "Mum gave me the tablets. She said they'd help."

"I think she knew they weren't helping, Red."

"You think she was doing it on purpose?" I nod. "Why?"

"Who rang social services? Who applied for the emergency care order? When Mav came by to check on you, she was reluctant to let him in. She didn't want him to see you like that because she knew he'd realise the truth."

Doc takes off his gloves. "All done. We'll get those swabs sent off to the lab, but I don't see any bruising down there, which is a good sign."

Rosey smiles reassuringly at me, but until the tests come back, I'm not convinced. "How will we know for sure?" I ask.

"In sexual assault cases, we'd usually find bruising in and around the vagina, maybe some bleeding even. There's nothing that concerns me. The swabs will show any STDs, and if you could provide a pee sample, we can check for bleeding." He hands Rosey a pot, and she gets up to go the bathroom.

"You sure she's not been touched?"

"As sure as I can be."

I head downstairs and relay the news to Mav, who's still holding church. The guys look relieved. "So, what was the point?" I throw out there. "If they didn't rape her, why were they keeping her drugged? Why was she naked?"

"Maybe they wanted to use her to get at you," suggests Ghost.

I shake my head. "They didn't know our connection. Rosey isn't one to tell everyone. Besides, when she went to them, we were over."

ALBERT

"It's not me they wanted." Rosey appears behind me. "They drugged me to keep me quiet. It's Ollie they want."

"Why?" asks Mav. "He's just a kid."

"And you're his family," says Rosey. "I think you're both the target."

ROSEY

I take a seat in the room and none of the bikers dare to question it. Mav smirks. "Come in, take a seat," he says with a hint of sarcasm.

"It's the easiest way to get to you," I continue. "You and the Taylors run this area, and they want it. He's already pushing drugs out under your nose by using kids."

"How do you know all this?" asks Grim.

"There are kids around their place all the time. It's obvious. He claims to be some kind of youth worker. I was sussing it all out when Mum gave me those pills. I think he realised I was on to him."

"And if the social worker confirms he got the ball rolling on the emergency care order, Rosey could be right," says Albert.

"We need a plan to get Ollie away from them," Grim says.

"I want in on the plans," I say firmly. "And I want to kill Dougie Harrison."

The following day, I wait anxiously by the window for the social worker. The second I see the car stop outside, I straighten my hair and head out to meet her. "Good morning," I say brightly, taking her by surprise. I hold out my hand, and she shakes it. "I'm Rosey. It's great to meet you."

Albert's car pulls in right behind hers and he gets out. "Sorry, I got held up at work," he apologises, rushing to stand at my side. "I'm Albert Taylor," he adds, also shaking her hand.

"You're looking much better from the last time I saw you," she tells me. "I'm Lucy Wells, the family support worker."

"You're not the social worker?" Albert asks.

"She called and asked me to come. She thought it would be better seeing as I'm acting in the whole family's interest. Jill was appointed as Ollie's social worker."

ALBERT

We head inside, and I point to the table where Mama B has laid out coffee and cake. We sit down, and I watch her take out a file. "You said you saw me before?" I ask.

Lucy smiles awkwardly. "I came along to visit with Jill. You were sleeping."

"I wasn't well..."

"It was five in the afternoon. Your mother told us you'd been in and out of that state for over a week."

"I had a virus," I continue. "It really knocked me off me feet."

"Your mother seemed to think it was more drug and alcohol related. She told us you have a history with addiction."

"Bullshit," snaps Albert. "That's not true. Connie's only been on the scene a short time. She doesn't even know Rosey."

I lay a hand over Albert's and shoot him a warning stare. I can't blow this, and I know how they take everything out of context. "I've been estranged from my mum for a long time. She wasn't the best parent. She has a history with addiction, and she's only known Ollie for a couple months."

"She gave you a place to stay?" Lucy asks, and I nod. "Rent free?" I nod again. "Because she was worried for Ollie."

"That's not true. I left here and planned to move away from the area. She convinced me to stay, and I offered money for the rent, but she refused to take it. I have money. I have plenty of it."

"Yet when we checked your cupboards, there was nothing in them. No food at all for Ollie."

"Because I got sick shortly after moving in. I hadn't had a chance to go shopping. Mum was taking care of him, so I wasn't worried."

"She told us that was never discussed. Ollie turned up on her doorstep upset because he was hungry."

I rack my brain. I don't remember Ollie being at home at all, so I certainly can't recall if he asked for food. "I was very sick. I don't remember Ollie asking for money or food. He knows how to order from his phone. He does it all the time."

"All the time?" she repeats.

I wince. "Not all the time. I meant he knows how to get food if he's hungry."

ALBERT

She scans her notes. "We spoke to the school. Ollie's attendance isn't good. He's had problems with behaviour, and they say they've tried to work with you, but you haven't been engaging with them, and you didn't show for the last couple of appointments."

I clench my jaw in frustration. "Like I said, I was sick. The school wanted to kick him out rather than work with me to help."

"Since the court order was granted in favour of your mother, Ollie's been in school every day. He's not caused any problems, and the teachers are delighted with his attitude to work. They've seen a real improvement."

I shake my head and sigh. "What's the point in me trying to convince you?" I ask, and she stares at me blankly. "You've made up your mind. My mother is no good. Her boyfriend is a drug dealer. He wants to use Ollie to get to this club. And if you don't start helping me, that's exactly what will happen."

She smiles awkwardly again. "We've spoken to Ollie. He's quite settled and happy with them."

"He's just telling you that because he's scared," Albert snaps. "Dougie threatened him." I glance at him, frowning. He never mentioned that. "He should be at home with his mum."

She places her file back in her bag. "I agree, Mr. Taylor. We do everything we can to keep families together. There's a court date in four weeks. Until then, we'd like you to take random drug tests three times a week. We'd also like you to provide a breath sample to check for alcohol."

I nod. "Of course, anything. When can I see Ollie?"

She stands. "We'll try and arrange something supervised."

"Supervised?" I repeat.

"It's part of the court order. Just standard procedure."

"What happened to innocent until proven guilty?" I snap.

"Jill visited you more than once, Rosey. Each time, you were out cold."

"And no one thought to check on her welfare?" snaps Albert.

"There were empty bottles and needles beside the bed. She wasn't even dressed appropriately."

I pull up my sleeves to show there are no track marks. "I don't use drugs," I tell her firmly. "I'm clean."

ALBERT

"Take the drugs tests. If the courts agree you're fit, they'll return Ollie into your care. I only have the evidence in front of me when these decisions are made. Unfortunately, the evidence showed that Ollie needed intervention. It doesn't mean it's forever. You have the power to change it."

"What about them? Do they have to take a test?" asks Albert.

She shakes her head. "Not unless you have proof they're using drugs."

I wait for her to go before turning to Albert. "Well, that's that then," I mutter helplessly.

"Four weeks," Albert mutters, running a hand through his hair. "We can't wait that long."

"If I can get Dougie away from Mum, she'll not be able to cope. She leans on a man for everything. Ollie could be placed with Maverick until the hearing. He is his brother," I suggest.

Albert nods. "Let's take it to Mav."

Mav listens, but when I get to the part where I go after Dougie, he shakes his head. "You're not strong enough right now, Rosey. You've been in bed for almost three weeks off your head."

"You owe me," I snap. "You both do," I add, glancing at Albert.

"This isn't about cashing in favours or trying to get one over on us because of Archer. We're looking out for you," Albert says.

"Get some food inside you. Rest. Then I'll get Grim in the basement with you. If you can take him down, I'll gladly let you go after Dougie."

"Grim will see me coming, Dougie won't—that's the beauty."

"You could always take a back-up," Albert suggests. "Lauren is on the books. I can get her to team up."

I stand, not bothering to respond to his ridiculous suggestion, and head out to the kitchen where I find Mama B stirring a pot of something delicious. I take a seat, and she eyes me before asking, "Are you okay?"

I nod. "Ever get tired of men telling you what to do?"

She laughs. "Depends. Are they telling you what to do because they're looking after you or because they're being bossy arseholes?"

I sigh. "I thought you might take Mav's side."

ALBERT

She laughs again. "I'm not on his side. I don't even know what you're talking about. But what I do know is he'll only ever do what's best for you."

"I just feel so useless sitting here while Ollie is there."

She stops stirring and pats my hand. "It must be hard, but you'll get him back. Mav and Albert will make sure of that."

"And what damage will be done before that happens?"

She begins to scoop what looks like soup into a bowl and slides it towards me. "Eat something. Think about your next move carefully, then take it back to Mav. No one can think straight on an empty stomach."

Chapter Fifteen

ALBERT

It's been a couple days since we had the visit from the family support worker. Rosey is making progress. She's eaten, or so Mama B tells me, because I haven't been around to watch for myself and now, as I watch her slip her hands into a set of boxing gloves, I realise she doesn't look as pale and tired as she did a few days ago.

Grim holds two pads up on his hands. "Go gentle. We don't want to overdo it," he warns, and she rolls her eyes.

"You're never around," says Meli as she leans against the tree nearby. "I thought you'd be glued to her side."

I've wanted to be. Every second I'm away from her, she consumes my mind. "She needs her space."

ALBERT

"Have you asked her if that's what she wants?"

"It's Rosey we're talking about. If she wanted me to stick around, she'd have told me."

Meli shakes her head sadly. "You have no idea, Albert. After everything, you still don't know how to deal with her."

"You don't deal with Rosey, she deals with you," I mutter, smirking.

"No. That's what she wants everyone to think, but it's not true. She's scared and heartbroken, just like any other woman would be after what she's been through. And you," she pushes off the tree and moves closer, "walked away when she needed you the most. You didn't notice the hurt you caused, and you walked away. So, now, she's guarding herself. Every night, when you walk away, she goes through the same hurt. She needs you, and you're not around. Be around, Albert. Stop walking away." She heads back towards the clubhouse, leaving me staring after her.

When Rosey is hot, sweaty, and tired, I step closer. "Enough," I say, and Grim nods in agreement. "Go and take a shower. We're going out for dinner," I tell her as Grim leaves us.

She hangs around nervously, keeping her eyes lowered. "I don't feel like leaving the clubhouse," she says.

I decide not to force the issue. "Fine, I'll bring dinner to you. Shower."

I put in a call to my favourite restaurant and offer double the price for a three-course meal to be delivered to the clubhouse. Then I enlist some of the prospects to set up a table outside. It's a warm night and it'll be nice to get away from the noise of the MC.

When the food arrives, I send Meli upstairs to find Rosey, and I wait outside, standing beside the table. When I see her step out, I light the candle and wait for her to join me. She eyes me suspiciously. "What are you doing?"

"I told you, we're having dinner." I pull out the seat for her, and she lowers into it. "I'd prefer a restaurant, but if you want to stay here, that's fine."

I lift the lid on her starter. Prawn cocktail is her favourite, and she smiles. "It looks delicious."

I take my seat and lift the lid on my own starter. She glances at my pâté longingly, and I roll my eyes, slicing some of it off and placing it on her plate. She grins. "I felt bad going out to eat when I don't know how Ollie is," she admits.

"Understandable."

"Mav's taking me to see him tomorrow." Mav had already mentioned it, but I let her tell me. "It's at the school and it's supervised, but it's better than nothing."

"Supervised is probably the best thing right now. That way, they can see how amazing you are with him. He'll be home before we know it."

"I hope so." We fall silent and then she asks, "So, you and Lauren, are you . . ." She trails off.

"Employer and employee," I finish the sentence. "I should have made that clear the night you turned up to dinner," I admit. "I was an idiot for letting you walk out of there under the impression we were more."

"It's fine."

"It's not fine, Red. I was a prick. I'm sorry. The truth is, we had a thing a long time ago, but I haven't thought about her since. We were kids, and it wasn't serious."

"Does she know that?" she asks with a small laugh.

"She's getting the message."

"You hurt me, Bert," she whispers, and I see that flash of vulnerability again. "A lot."

I place my fork down and take her hand. "I know. I underestimated how much. You're just so strong all the time, and I thought you'd be okay. You act like you don't give a crap..."

"That's all it is, an act," she admits, then she takes a shaky breath. "All my life is an act. I don't even know who the real me is anymore."

"Maybe we can find out together," I suggest with hope in my voice.

"I'd like that," she almost whispers.

We move on to the main course, and she groans when she sees the steak. "It's the size of a cow."

"It's good for you," I tell her. "Lots of red meats will help build your strength."

"That's all Mama B has said to me these last few days. I swear, I'll be the size of a house if you all keep ramming food down my throat." We fall silent for a few minutes, and I watch her pop a piece of steak into her mouth before closing her eyes and humming her approval. "Do you think Ollie will want to see me tomorrow?" she asks, suddenly looking vulnerable again.

I nod, cutting into my steak. "Why wouldn't he?"

She shrugs. "Maybe he'll blame me for letting them take him."

ALBERT

"He's not stupid, Red. He'll know it was out your hands."

"They'll be my last kill," she eventually adds. "Then I'm done with that part of my life."

"You think that's wise?" I ask. "Mav can deal with them. It'll look less suspicious if you don't know any of the details."

"They crossed me and my boy, I'm taking them out. I need them to see my face as they take their last breaths and know they fucked with the wrong person."

I nod in understanding. She's got a thirst for their blood, and I don't blame her. I'd be the same. "It's gotta go down right, Rosey. It can't lead back to you."

She scoffs. "I'd happily do time for them."

"And then Ollie would be without his mum. I'm serious, Rosey. Don't go off and deal with this on your own. You have everyone at the club as well as me and Art behind you. You don't have to do this shit alone."

We move on to dessert, a delicate chocolate fondu, and as we finish, she throws her napkin down. "Maybe you could come tomorrow? Maybe just wait outside?" I'm happy she's asked, so I nod. "It's at nine in the morning. You'll need to be up early."

"You can wake me," I tell her, standing and holding out my hand for her to take. She frowns. "I thought I'd stay with you tonight, if that's okay." She lowers her head to hide the smile, and I lead her inside.

We shower separately, and by the time I join her in her bedroom, she's sitting in bed watching television. She tugs the sheet back for me to climb in, and once I do, she snuggles against me. It's a first and I can't stop the smile spreading across my face as I place my arm around her. This feels good, like it's where I was always meant to be.

I tip her head back by placing my finger under her chin so we're eye to eye. "No more running, Rosey," I say firmly.

Her eyes flick away briefly, and when they return to mine, I see a subtle change there. She smiles. "No more running."

I place my lips against hers, feeling a rush of relief spread through my body. Hearing her say the words is like a weight has been lifted. Maybe, finally, we'll stop this merry dance of denial and we can move forward. Her hand cups my cheek and she deepens the kiss. After a few moments, I begin to pull back, not wanting her to think I'm after anything from her right now except love and comfort, but she throws the sheets back and climbs onto my lap, kissing me again. "I've missed you," she whispers against my mouth. It's words I never thought I'd hear from her guarded self.

"I missed you too, so fucking much."

"Show me," she adds, gently rocking against my now solid erection. I close my eyes, allowing myself to enjoy the feel of her body against mine.

"Shouldn't we take things slow?" I query.

She shakes her head, biting on her lower lip and lifting her shirt over her head to reveal her naked breasts. "Slow is for new couples, and we're way past that." I grin as she pushes up onto her knees so she can reach inside my boxers. "We're practically married," she adds, fisting my cock.

I still her hand. "If we're doing this, we're doing it my way for a change," I tell her, gripping her by the waist and rolling so she's beneath me. "We're not fucking." I kiss her until her breath catches, and then I begin to run my mouth down her body, nipping and licking as I go. I settle between her legs, "I'm taking my time," I add, swiping my tongue through her folds, and her back arches off the bed. "I want to taste every inch of you." I seal my mouth over her, sucking until she cries out in pleasure. "I want to hear you call my name," I murmur, "every time I make you come." She grips a handful of the sheet, groaning as I continue torturing her slowly. When she finally comes, it's with my name on her lips.

ROSEY

I know what he's doing as he slides up my body, occasionally stopping to kiss my damp skin. He's making love. It's different from our other times, and I'm not freaking out like I thought I would. I want him to take his time. I want to relax in his arms while he takes care of me.

He lines his erection up at my entrance, and as he slides into me, he places gentle kisses over my face. He withdraws just as slowly, this time looking into my eyes with a deep intensity that sends shivers down my spine. His lips find mine and the kiss is soft and breathy, breaking each time he fills me. He rests his forehead against my own, our heavy breathing mingling together in gasps of pleasure, and when I come for a second time, he follows me over the edge, groaning somewhere deep in the back of his throat.

He drops down beside me, wrapping me in his arms and pulling me against his body.

I wake with a nervous feeling inside. Albert is still wrapped around me, and I carefully unwrap his arms and slip out of bed, heading for the shower. I'm seeing Ollie in just over an hour and I want to be there early to show commitment.

Albert is still in a deep sleep when I'm dressed, so I head downstairs for breakfast, where the dining room is its usual chaotic self. I sit down beside Hadley and reach for some toast. "Big day today," she says, pouring me a coffee.

"Why do I feel so nervous?" I ask.

She smiles, placing her hand over mine. "It's all going to be fine. Ollie will be home with us in no time at all."

"You think?" I ask, glancing at her.

She nods. "We'll build a big case against your mum, discrediting her. If they really want to go down that road, we'll be ready for them. See how today goes, but I think we should at least have Maverick go for temporary custody."

I scoff. "I've been thinking about that. I don't think they'll ever give Ollie to Maverick. The judge will see he's a biker and throw it right out."

Hadley smiles knowingly. "A man who helps the community, gives back to society, and rescues domestic abuse survivors. We'll have the judge begging him to take Ollie."

Maverick stands. "You ready to go?" he asks.

I nod, following his lead and heading out for the car. Albert is leaning against it, looking at his mobile. My heart fills with hope, and when he looks up and smiles, I return it. "I hope you didn't think you could sneak off without me."

"You looked so peaceful in bed, I didn't want to wake you."

He kisses me on the cheek. "That's because I finally got a good night's sleep with you by my side, where you belong."

We drive in silence to the school, and as we pull up in the car park, Albert turns to face me. "Do you want us to come in with you?" I appreciate him giving me the choice and I nod. I don't think I can face this alone.

The headteacher is waiting in the reception area, talking quietly with Ollie's social worker. Mrs. Ball smiles warmly. "Rosey, this is Jill, Ollie's social worker." We shake hands.

ALBERT

"I hope it's okay, I brought Kilian Maverick, Ollie's half-brother. And this is my . . ." I pause, wondering how to introduce Albert, but he steps forward, holding out his hand.

"Albert Taylor, Rosey's partner." I smile, enjoying how the words sound coming from him.

We're shown into the office where Ollie is waiting. My heart pounds in my chest, and he stands, rushing to me and embracing me. Relief floods me. I've been so worried he'd not want to see me or he'd blame me for his situation, I hadn't allowed myself to relax and think he's been missing me as much as I've been missing him.

I pull back slightly and brush his messy hair from his eyes. "How are you?"

"I want to come home," he mutters, still holding onto me. "I'm so sorry for being a shit."

"Don't curse," I say, kissing him on the cheek. "And this isn't because of you, Ollie. This is my fault for trusting Mum again."

"If we could avoid talking about the situation," Jill interrupts, and I glare at her.

"You don't want me to explain to him that it isn't his fault?"

"Of course, it's fine, but let's not discuss Ollie's current carers."

"I respect you, your job is hard," I say, trying to remain calm, "but trust me when I say you have this whole situation wrong."

"We can discuss that away from Ollie, after your visit," she says firmly.

I take a seat beside Ollie. Mav, Albert, and Mrs. Ball step out of the office, leaving me alone with him and Jill. "What have you been doing?" I ask, taking his hand and stroking it gently.

"Nothing. Nan said I can't leave the flat apart from going to school."

I frown, glancing at Jill to see her making notes. "Why?"

"She's scared you'll come and take me, or I'll run back to the clubhouse."

"As much as I would love that, you know you can't. Hadley is sorting it. I'm really trying to get you home where you belong."

"Will it take long?"

I shrug. "I don't know how long these things take. I hope not."

"Dougie said Nan should go for full custody."

ALBERT

I sigh. "I don't know why he's encouraging it. It doesn't make sense."

"Am I allowed to speak to Maverick?" Ollie asks Jill, and she nods. "I mean alone. Without you or Mum?"

She ponders it before nodding. "I don't see why not. He's not down as needing supervised access. I'll give you five minutes with him at the end."

"What happens next?" I ask.

"There's a multiagency meeting after this. We'll discuss Ollie's needs and if you've been meeting them and what you'd need to do to meet them."

"I didn't know about the meeting," I say, confused.

"Lucy was supposed to inform you. I know she's been busy. It's in the school, if you're free to stay on?"

"Of course."

Mav puts a call into Hadley, asking her to join us in the meeting. He then spends five minutes alone with Ollie, but he's unable to fill me in because the meeting is directly after and we're called into a bigger room where the headteacher, Jill, Lucy, me, and Maverick sit around the table.

Hadley bursts in five minutes late, but they allow it seeing as they never told me about the meeting.

Jill begins by telling me that Ollie seems happy and settled at his nan's. She's provided new clothes for him and is decorating her bedroom for him to stay in. "Why is she doing that?" I ask. "He isn't staying there."

"In case this becomes a longer-term thing," Jill replies.

"I've been busy this morning," says Hadley, opening her bag and pulling out some documents. "And I managed to do a check on Dougie Harrison. I assume you ran a thorough check on him?" she asks Jill, who looks flustered for a second before bridging her fingers and leaning forward.

"We're very stretched at the moment. The check was requested, but I haven't had a chance to look through my emails to see if it's been returned."

Hadley opens the envelope and pulls out some paperwork. "Let me save you the job. Dougie used to go by the name Lee Harrison. He went to prison for assault on his ex-wife. That was thirty years ago. He served five years and, upon his release, he tracked her down and beat her to death." I inhale sharply, my head beginning to swim with panic. "He was sent back to prison for fifteen years for that.

He served twelve and was released for good behaviour. Can you believe that?" She looks up, then smiles coldly at Jill.

Maverick scoffs. "Not the first time we've seen men like him released early."

"Anyway, he changed his name to Darren Harrison and spent the next few years off-radar. Another name change to Dougie and he came to London six years ago, where he became a youth worker."

"We don't discriminate against people who have turned their life around," Jill mutters.

"Youth worker is his disguise," Hadley continues. "He's a big-time dealer on the estate where he lives, using kids to run his drugs around to dealers."

"Have you got any proof?" Jill asks.

"Are you shitting me?" I snap. "Get my kid out of there right now. Proof or not, he's got a criminal record."

"Your mother is ultimately the one who decided to provide temporary custody," she tells me.

"He's living there."

"She told me he has his own place. It's a one-bedroom flat and Ollie is in the bedroom. There's no room for Dougie."

"You'd rather my son be around a murderer than me? I love my son. Whatever you saw when you came by to visit was because of him and my mother. You know she used to sell herself to men when I was little? She left me alone all the time to fuck men for money."

Hadley pats my hand, and I press my lips together. "We'd like to offer a suggestion," she says.

"I'm listening."

"We won't file a complaint about this little mess if Ollie is placed with a better option temporarily."

"Such as?"

"Me or Kilian. We're half-related—our father is Ollie's father. I'm a solicitor for a top law firm in London, and Kilian is an upstanding member of the community, providing safe houses and support to women leaving abusive situations. I can offer you full background checks on us both to save you messing this up further."

"But you live with Rosey. Ollie can't have unsupervised access," Jill points out.

"I'll move out," I jump in quickly. "I'll stay somewhere else."

Jill looks to Lucy, who shrugs. "I'm not sure a judge could approve this before the weekend. It might have to wait until Monday."

"I can get that sorted too," says Hadley, looking smug. "I can put a call in to Judge Earl Morris. He's sitting today until six p.m. Let me put the call in, and we can have the paperwork emailed by the end of the day."

Maverick leans forward. "I don't see you have a choice. If the press heard about this charade of you not doing background checks for a child you already consider to be vulnerable," he shakes his head, "they'd eat you alive. Aren't you already in special measures?"

Jill sighs. "Fine, let me run it past my boss." She stands, pulling out her phone and stepping out the office.

Lucy smiles warmly. "Where will you go, Rosey?"

"Albert will arrange it," Maverick cuts in.

"You know social services may do drop-ins to check you're not there."

I nod. "I won't be there. I'll know he's safe with these two, so I can relax."

Jill returns. "If you can get a judge to sign it off, go ahead. We'll need the full address of where Ollie will be staying too."

Hadley collects her things together. "I'll go and sort it right away. We'll look forward to having Ollie home tonight."

She leaves, and I turn to Jill. "What happens now? Will Ollie be going back to my mum's?"

"If the paperwork is with me by six, I'll drive him to collect his things and take him to the address provided to the judge." I relax slightly, knowing at least Ollie will be away from that bitch for now. "We'll arrange another visit next week."

"When will I be able to have him with me?" I ask.

"We need to see clear drug and alcohol tests, which Lucy will take care of. We need to see a home that's stable for him, and once he returns to you, we'll have to monitor the situation to check he's doing well and things don't deteriorate."

Chapter Sixteen

ALBERT

I stop the car outside the double black gates and press a button for them to open. Rosey leans forward, looking at the white house as I drive up towards it. "Whose house is this?" she asks.

I stop the car and get out, rounding her side and opening her door. "Do you like it?" I ask, keeping hold of her hand and leading her up the steps.

"Yeah, it's stunning. This area is so expensive. Are you breaking in?"

I laugh and produce the front door key. "Nope, I have full permission to be here." I unlock the door and lead her into the hall. It was the first thing I loved about it when I saw it. The wide staircase curves off and the hall is huge. I put the code in to deactivate the alarm. "Shoes," I tell her, and we both kick them off.

I lead her through to the kitchen, the second room that sold this place to me. I watch as she stares in awe at the kitchen island and the new units. "It's so modern."

"Drink?" I ask, taking the kettle and filling it with water.

"Are you going to tell me who owns this place and why we're here?"

"You need a place to show the social worker, right?"

She laughs. "Yeah, but it needs to be a permanent place. They'll be around for a while keeping an eye on things. Besides, once I'm allowed, I'll go back to the clubhouse."

I take her hand and pull her closer. "I thought about this long and hard," I say, tucking her hair away from her face, "and I thought it was about time you had a place to call your own. A place to settle and put down roots. A place with me . . ." I trail off, and Rosey stares at me open-mouthed. "Is it too much?" I ask, suddenly feeling ridiculous. Arthur warned me not to rush anything. "Fuck, I've messed this up, haven't I? Look, if you hate the idea, I'll sell it. Or I can just stay where I am, and you and Ollie can live here."

She grabs my face and stands on her tiptoes. "Stop talking," she whispers. Then she kisses me hard, wrapping her arms around my neck. I tug her closer, lifting her legs and wrapping them around my waist. We're panting when we pull apart. "No one's ever done anything like this for me," she says against my mouth. "You bought us a house?"

I nod, smiling. "So, you're happy, not mad?"

She kisses me again. "Really happy."

We get the call from Mav to confirm Ollie is now in his and Hadley's care. Rosey is so relieved, she almost cries. "Now he's out of there, I can pay them a visit," she says.

I gently pull her to me. "I don't think that's a good idea. We know nothing about Dougie, not really. We should do more research. Mav is putting some guys on him to watch his movements."

"He uses kids to run his drugs, that tells me all I need to know."

"Rosey, I'm serious about this. Let's do our homework." She nods in agreement, but there's a look in her eye that tells me she isn't leaving this until she's at least spoken with her mum.

I eventually leave Rosey to get settled in, then I head to the clubhouse to collect some of her clothes. Ollie rushes over when he spots me. "Is Mum with you?" he asks eagerly.

I shake my head, and he looks disappointed. "She isn't allowed around you without your social worker giving her the nod. She'd be here if she could, you know that." I follow him over to the couch. "I actually wanted to speak to you," I add, sitting beside him. "I wanted to run something by you." He looks wary. "Well, you're the only man in your mum's life that she'd do anything for, so I thought it was important to run things by you." He relaxes a little. "I bought a place," I begin, "somewhere for you and your mum to settle." I pull out my phone and bring up some pictures of the house. "It's not far from the clubhouse, so you'll get to see Mav all the time."

He takes my phone and examines the pictures closely. "Will I have a big bedroom?"

I nod. "Huge."

"Can I have a game set up in there?"

I smirk. "If your mum says that's okay."

ALBERT

He hands my phone back to me. "Okay. Cool."

"The thing is—"

"I'm not calling you dad," he cuts in, and I try to hide my smile. "Cos that would be weird. And I don't want to see you kissing and stuff. Don't gross me out." I nod. "But it's cool if you're moving in too. I think you make Mum happy."

"I try."

"Don't make her sad. Ever."

I nod again. "Understood."

He stands. "I'll send you some pictures of the computer set-up." And then he wanders off.

My shoulders relax and I release a long breath. "What's up with you?" asks Mav, joining me. "You look relieved."

"I was dreading having that chat with Ollie, yet he handled it really well."

"About the house?" he asks.

"I thought he'd hate the idea."

"He's a good kid. He also gave me a long list of names Dougie Harrison associates with, none of which are of any concern to us. Not one big name in there. He lets the young kids on the estate run his packages to dealers. He's a small-time idiot thinking he's going places."

I check my watch. "Well, I can promise you it's not going to last. I'll bet money Rosey is already on her way over there to settle a score."

Mav groans. "I thought we were gonna watch and wait?"

"Try telling her that. You know she doesn't listen to anyone. But she's got this, and she needs to settle things her way."

ROSEY

I pull up my hood and take a seat on the brick wall opposite the block of flats Mum lives in. The usual kids are racing around on bikes, and I wonder how many of them are carrying drugs for that prick. My mobile rings, and I get it out my pocket and smile when I see Albert's name. "We've been apart for half an hour, what could you possibly need?" I ask when I answer.

"Just to hear your voice. You all good?"

"Yep, just chilling," I lie.

He laughs. "Rosey, let's not start our journey together on lies. Just don't get yourself arrested. I love you."

I smile wider. "I love you too." I disconnect and stare up at the door to my mum's place. A kid is just leaving, and I keep my eyes fixed on him until he's back on ground level.

ALBERT

I make my way over, placing my hand on his handlebars just as he's about to get on his bike. "Give it to me," I say, and he frowns.

"Aren't you Ollie's mum?"

"Give me the package."

He glances around for backup, but it's getting dark and this isn't the sort of place where people wander around. "I can't, I'll get hurt if I do."

"By the time I'm done, there will be nobody left to hurt you, so hand it over." He groans, pulling out a neatly taped package. "Now, go home and look after your mum instead of being part of this bullshit."

"I need the money," he snaps.

I hand him one of Mav's business cards. "You wanna earn, do it honestly. This guy can help. Just tell him Rosey sent you."

I let him go and head around the back of the flats where a lot of homeless people hang out. There are some bin fires going, but I settle away from them all and pull out everything I need. I spend the next twenty minutes heating up the heroin and sucking it into syringes. When I'm done, I take the rest of the package and throw it in a nearby fire bin, smiling as it goes up in flames.

I take the concrete steps two at a time until I'm outside Mum's flat. Inhaling deeply, I release it slowly and move my head from side to side before shaking my shoulders to relax myself. I push the door and walk inside, then I gently push the kitchen door open. It's in darkness, so I move to the bedroom where Dougie is sleeping butt naked with his arms above his head, perfectly in position. I grin.

Gently, I put a pull tie around each wrist, then connect the two with another tie. He doesn't even stir, so I continue on to the living room, where Mum is staring blankly at the television. She catches my movement and turns to face me, looking surprised. "Rosey."

"Surprise."

"You can't be here. Dougie won't be happy about it."

"Why? What exactly did I do?"

"What with all the business with Ollie, he just . . ."

"I mean what exactly did I do to you, Mum? What did I do to make you hate me so much?"

She looks away. "I don't hate you, Rosey."

"It feels like hate," I say, shrugging out of my jacket but leaving my gloves in place. She eyes me warily.

"What the fuck?" yells Dougie, and she suddenly looks panicked.

"You need to go," she hisses.

"Connie, are you into some kinky shit?" he shouts, stumbling into the room still naked. His eyes fall to me and turn to anger. "What the fuck is she doing here?"

I grin, and as he makes his way to me, I raise my foot and push it against his stomach, causing him to fall back into the chair. "Now, now, Dougie, you don't look at all pleased to see me."

"Did you do this?" he growls, holding up his bound hands.

I wince. "Sorry, did you think Mum was about to perform for you?"

"Rosey, stop all this," Mum snaps. "What's gotten into you?"

"Did I ever tell you what my job was?" I ask, wandering over to the mantel and running my finger along the dusty shelf. "Of course not. I mean, you probably never asked, did you? If it isn't about you, you don't want to know."

"Don't be ridiculous."

"What do you know about my life, Mum?" I ask, turning to face her.

Dougie tries to get up, but I shove him back. He glares angrily. "I don't know what the fuck you think you're gonna do, little girl, but when I get out of these, you're one dead bitch."

I smile, patting him on the head. "Relax, stepdaddy dearest, it'll all be over soon."

The front door bangs and Dice saunters in. "What are you doing here?" I snap.

He grins, leaning on the door frame. "Mav sent me, said you might need a hand."

I scowl. "Well, I don't."

"It's about time I crashed one of your jobs," he says, and I groan.

I turn back to Mum. "Ignore him. I was about to tell you what I did for my job."

"How does your mum not know what you do for a living?" Dice asks.

"What the fuck is going on?" Dougie yells in frustration.

"She'll drag this out, so get used to it," Dice explains. "She can never just end things—it's got to be theatrical."

"End things?" repeats Dougie, laughing. "What the fuck can she do to end me?"

Dice grins. "Fuck, they really don't know you, do they?"

ALBERT

I pull out the syringes and lay them on the table. "People pay me to rid the world of negative influences."

Dice snort-laughs. "Is that an official job title?"

"And you, Dougie, are a very negative influence. Why exactly were you so desperate to have my son?"

"Kids like him are crying out for male attention," he spits. "It didn't take long to have him working for me. He told me about his mum never being around, and then I found out he was Connie's grandson. I've spent months hearing how you treat your mum, and it was about time you saw how hard parenting can be."

I frown. "You wanted to teach me a lesson?"

"I wanted to take the streets from The Perished Riders. Ollie was my way in."

"How?"

"Like I'm gonna tell you. You might think you've won, but when we take our evidence to court, the judge will hand Ollie right back over to his grandmother."

"Evidence?" asks Dice.

"And if anything happens to me, they'll come right to the club," he adds, smirking.

"Bullshit," I mutter, picking up a syringe. "Yah know what I just found? A whole lot of shit you were about to push out on the street."

"And you didn't touch it, right?" he growls. "Cos if it doesn't get to where it's going, we have a problem."

"*We* don't," I tell him. "*You* do." I grab his arm, and he tries to shrug me off. Dice takes over, pulling his arms down and holding them steady while I tie one off and wait for a vein to pop up. "Don't you trust your own shit?" I ask.

"I'm not a user," he yells.

"Rosey, stop," cries Mum.

"I'm just doing my job, Mum. Did you tell him to stop when he was giving me pills?"

I press the needle to his vein until it breaks the skin. "Enjoy the ride," I whisper, plunging the heroin into him.

He relaxes, letting his head fall back. "Did you?" I ask her again. "Each pill he shoved down my throat, did you ask him to stop?" She looks uncomfortable. "Because that's your one job as a mother," I continue, "to protect your child, and I don't remember you ever doing that for me."

"I found it hard," she whispers. "Being a mum didn't come naturally to me."

"Nor me," I yell, pushing my face closer to hers, "because I had no one to teach me. But what I did have was a whole load of memories telling me what not to do." Dice steps out the room. "For instance, I never had sex with anyone while Ollie was in the room. You can ask Ollie if he's ever heard me have sex and I can promise you he'll say no."

"What is this achieving, Rosey?"

I shrug. "I guess it makes me feel better. Another parenting no-no is getting so wasted on drink and drugs that your kid has to put you to bed and clean up your vomit."

"Please, just stop," she whispers.

"And yet you thought you'd be a better parent to my son than me?"

"I've changed."

"No, you haven't. You still repeat the same cycles—bad choices in men, letting them do what they want, and letting them harm me."

"You were depressed. You needed medicating," she argues.

"Is that what he told you?" I yell. "Did that make it easier to believe you were doing something good? I came to you for help, and that doesn't happen often, but because I've been there for you a million times, I thought I could trust you to be there for me." I take a shuddering breath. "Just one time, Mum. I just needed you one time."

"I was trying to help."

"Bullshit. You wanted my son because Dougie told you that's what you wanted. You could have told him to fuck off, Mum. I was happy to have you in mine and Ollie's life again, but it wasn't enough, was it? It's never enough for you because you need a man to live, to breathe, to exist."

"You were hard work growing up. It was easier to have help than be on my own."

"Do you know how those men helped, Mum? They fucked me. I was a kid and you let that happen. Do you remember the talk back when Eagle was in charge of the club, and you told me I couldn't expect to live for free? That I had to pay my way the same as every other woman there?"

"It was just the way."

"I was a kid," I yell again. "You should have paid my way, but no, they wanted me, and you let them take me."

"I was trying to survive. Eagle said he'd kick us out in the street."

ALBERT

"Then you should have packed our things and walked away. Everything you've ever done has been about you. I won't be here for you again. I won't let Ollie watch this messed-up relationship."

"Do you really kill people?" she whispers.

I nod. "Yep. You can take the credit for that too, if you like. I got sick of men using me, and I was terrified I'd end up like you. See, I don't need a man, not for money, not for sex, and not to fight my battles."

"So, why is Albert Taylor on the scene?" she asks smugly. "Rich man with a nasty streak . . . you're exactly like me."

I laugh. "He's around because I allow him to be. And I don't need his money, I have plenty of my own."

I insert another syringe into Dougie, but he doesn't stir as I top up his hit. "You'll kill him," Mum spits.

"I know. That's the plan."

"Is that what you're going to do to me?" she asks.

I shrug. "I haven't decided."

"I'm happy to help if needed," says Dice from the kitchen.

I smile. "You don't kill women, remember?"

"For you, I would," he says, and it almost warms my cold heart.

I place a syringe closer to Mum. "I want you to make the choice."

"You want me to decide if I want to die?" She laughs, but it's cold and empty. "I remember a time you'd beg me not to die, and trust me, I wanted to. You made me stay," she spits.

I shrug, pointing to the needle. "I'm not going to stop you now, Mum. I see you're in pain, and it's the sort of pain that'll never leave because it's in your heart and your mind. You're so fucking messed up, you'll never get well again. So, if you want to leave, I'm not stopping you."

"You want me dead so I can't tell anyone what you just did to Dougie," she snaps.

"The least you owe me as my mother is to keep your mouth shut. You've done fuck all else for me."

"And you trust me, do you? With that huge secret?"

"God, no. I'll never trust you again after what you did to me and Ollie, but if the police come for me, someone will come for you. You think Albert Taylor won't slit your throat if you take away his woman?"

I put another needle into Dougie's arm. It's the final dose that'll end his life, and as he begins to convulse, I step back, watching him shake violently while foaming at the

ALBERT

mouth. Mum begins to cry and turns away. "What do I tell the police?"

"That you came home to find him like this." I remove the first two syringes, leaving just one hanging from his arm. "They'll think he took a fatal dose."

"What if they think I had something to do with it?" she asks.

I shrug. "Honestly, I don't care."

Chapter Seventeen

ALBERT

I swirl the amber liquid around my glass. "You weren't home," says Rosey, approaching the bar. She takes a seat on the stool beside me.

"Sounds good," I tell her, smiling, "when you say it like that."

"Vodka, neat," she tells the barman.

"Do I need to ask where you've been?"

She takes her drink, knocking it back in one. "There were some loose ends to tie up."

I take a piece of her hair and wrap it around my finger. "Are those ends tied?"

"Almost," she replies. "Let's go home."

ALBERT

We're awoken by a knock at the door. I stretch out, looking around and realising we're in our new home. Rosey stirs beside me, and I run my hand over her naked arse. I spent most the night worshipping her body, so it's no surprise we're both still in bed. I pull on some joggers and rush down to answer the door, where I find two police officers. My heart stutters. "Mr. Taylor?"

"That's me."

"We're looking for Rosey White."

"She's asleep. Is it urgent?"

He nods. "It's about her mother, Connie White."

I let them in and show them to the kitchen. As I approach the stairs, Rosey is already descending, rubbing her sleepy eyes. "You didn't wake me."

"There're some visitors," I whisper. "Two police officers. They said it was regarding your mum."

She suddenly looks alert but takes a deep calming breath before pasting a worried look on her face. I follow her back into the kitchen. "What's going on?" she asks.

"We're very sorry, Miss White, but your mother was found dead this morning in her flat."

Rosey grabs on to the kitchen worktop to support herself. "Dead? How?"

"It seems she overdosed on heroin. She left a note," he says, handing her a clear plastic evidence bag.

Rosey takes it and scans it before handing it back. "It doesn't surprise me. She's been hanging around with some bad people. She was bound to fall into old habits eventually."

"Yes, she was found with Dougie Harrison. He had also overdosed."

Rosey rolls her eyes. "She probably did it to be with him. The old cow never could live without a man."

"A full autopsy will be carried out at the coroner's request, but we're not looking for anybody else."

I place an arm around Rosey's shoulders and kiss her gently on the head. "I'll show you out," I tell them before leading them to the exit.

When I go back to the kitchen, Rosey is making coffee and humming to herself. "Are you okay?" I ask.

"Tiptop," she singsongs.

ALBERT

"Was she alive when you left her last night?" I ask cautiously.

She pauses to look at me. "What do you take me for, a monster? I'd never kill my own mother." She goes back to humming.

"So, what happened?"

"You heard the officer, she overdosed."

I round the kitchen island and take her hand, halting her coffee making. "Rosey, you're not alone anymore. We can talk about this shit."

She lowers her eyes. "I told you they'd be my last kill, Bert. Dougie was no accident. Mum had a choice, and I guess she chose the easy option."

"Are you upset?"

She shakes her head. "I thought I might be, but actually, I'm calm."

"What did the note say?"

"I'm choosing to leave."

"Do those words mean anything to you?" I ask.

"I told her she had a choice, to stay or leave. That's my answer."

I place a kiss on her head. "I'm sorry, baby," I whisper.

"Ollie needs to know. Should I wait or get Mav to tell him?"

"I'll tell him," I say. "If that's okay with you."

Ollie is out front with Mav, looking over a motorbike. I'd rang ahead to inform Mav about our morning visit from the police. He didn't seem surprised either. He spots me and pats Ollie on the back, so he also looks up. We shake hands. "Does Mum like the house?" he asks.

I smile, nodding. "But that's not what I'm here about," I tell him.

Mav guides him to the wall, and we sit down. "We had a visit from the police this morning. Apparently, your nan and Dougie took an overdose last night."

Ollie stares wide-eyed. "Are they okay?"

I shake my head. "Your mum wanted to be here to tell you all this herself, but we couldn't get hold of Jill to clear it. They passed away, Ollie. I'm so sorry."

Instead of upset, I'm met with relief. "Can I come home now?"

ALBERT

I glance at Mav, who squeezes Ollie's shoulder. "It's not that simple, Olls, but I'm sure it won't be long."

ROSEY

By Monday, I'm feeling sad. Not about Mum—she hasn't entered my head since I found out she died—but I'm missing Ollie, and the more time I spend in our new house, the more I want him here. It feels empty without him.

Meli comes rushing in and throws her arms around me. "How was the holiday?" I ask. She'd convinced Arthur to whisk her away for the third time this year.

"Oh my god, this house is perfect," she cries, looking around the kitchen. "I go away for a little break and all hell is breaking loose here. Albert just told us about Connie."

I shrug. "I'm not upset. I'm relieved." She goes to the coffee pot and switches it on. I smile as she checks the cupboards for cups, then I sit down and let her make the coffees. "I've spent so long worrying about her, it's nice to know I don't have to anymore."

She joins me with two steaming cups. "Really? Don't you feel just a little bit sad?"

I wrap my hands around the cup. "The day I found out she was gone, my mood was low, but not because of her death. It was because I sat and thought about all the bad times. I couldn't think of one good one, Meli, not one. I remember sitting in a bathroom once, it smelt so bad and I was there for hours, just sitting on the floor because she told me to wait in there while she fucked her way around an MC. She never cared about me. I was just an inconvenience to her. The first home I had, was with you, Mav, and Hadley, and even that had monsters. I've never truly felt safe, not until I killed Eagle. That's the day I knew that one day, she'd have to die too. I'm just glad she made the right decision for once and did it before I was forced to."

She squeezes my hand gently. "And what about Ollie? Any news?"

"They want me to do random tests to prove I'm not a drunk or an addict. I have to jump through hoops just to see him." My phone rings. "Speaking of hoops," I mutter before pressing it to my ear. "Hey, Lucy."

"Rosey, I'm so sorry to hear about your mum. Are you okay?"

ALBERT

"It's hard," I lie, "but at least she isn't suffering anymore. I'm more worried about Ollie. I want to be there for him, and I can't."

"That's why I'm calling. Can you drop by the office? I have something to show you."

Half an hour later, Meli and I enter the family services office where Lucy is waiting for me. She ushers us into a room. "I got into work today to find this," she says, holding up a brown envelope. "You need to see this," she adds, grabbing her laptop and turning it towards us.

An image fills the screen of me passed out on a bed. I recognise the flat I was staying in that Dougie had rented out to me. I'm naked, and Mum is standing over me. Dougie comes into view and lifts my head up by my hair. He pushes a pill into my mouth and drops my head back down. "Are you sure this is the right way to do things?" Mum asks.

"Don't you want to teach the little bitch a lesson, Connie? She treats you like crap. She doesn't deserve Ollie. We've been over this."

"He doesn't deserve this. He's worried about her."

"He's a kid, but once I'm done with him, he'll be a man. He can own these streets once I'm too old to carry on. We're giving him a future."

"When The Perished Riders find out about it, they might come for us."

"By then, it'll be too late. We'll hold Ollie over them until they back the fuck off."

Lucy closes the laptop. "I don't know who sent this, but it's also filming when we came to visit and you were out of it. Dougie is seen right before we arrive, giving you more pills."

Meli grabs my hand. "So, it proves that Rosey wasn't lying. She didn't take the pills."

Lucy nods. "I'm waiting on a call back from Jill, but I don't see why we have to keep you and Ollie apart any longer. Your drug tests came back clear, as did the alcohol. Social services might want to keep checking in before you're fully discharged, but I doubt they'll be around for long."

A tear rolls down my cheek. Mum must have sent this in. Who else would have recorded that? The office phone rings and Lucy answers. She relays her evidence to Jill before hanging up. "She agrees. We'll call your solicitor, Hadley, was it?" I nod. "See if that judge can't reverse the care order."

Albert takes my hand, and we rest against his car. Kids pour out of the school gates, and I scan them for Ollie. When I finally see him, I wave frantically, and he looks mortified. Albert laughs, tugging my arm down as Ollie heads over. "What are you doing here?" he asks, glancing around.

"I got some good news," I tell him. "You can come home."

His eyes widen in surprise. "Really?" I nod. He throws his arms around me, suddenly not caring if his friends see or not. I inhale his musky aftershave and the teenage smell that is all Ollie, and I relax.

We get home shortly after, and Albert wastes no time rushing upstairs with Ollie hot on his heels to show him the new bedroom he had done. It's got all the latest computer equipment and the best LED lights, all requested by

Ollie. And I know it means so much to Albert that Ollie feels settled here.

When Albert returns to the kitchen twenty minutes later, he's grinning. "I take it he liked it?" I ask.

"He loved it. He said it's the best room he's ever had. He also invited me to play a game on his PC later. It looks violent."

I laugh. "And what did you say?"

"I told him his mother was abandoning us to see her girls later, so a night on the computer sounds fantastic."

"I didn't make plans," I say, frowning.

"I made plans. You need this, and I need time to bond with Ollie. I've never been a dad before, especially to a teenager, and I don't want to mess it up."

I wrap my arms around him, placing kisses along his jaw. "I love you, Mr. Taylor," I whisper.

"Remember my rule," comes Ollie's voice.

I smile against Albert's mouth. "I make the rules around here, kid," I tell him.

ALBERT

It's been so long since all the old ladies got together, that for once, I'm excited to be around people. Albert arranged for us to take one of the VIP areas in Bertie's with drinks on the house. "Ghost wasn't impressed when Mav gave us the go-ahead to leave the club unescorted," Nelly tells me as she refills my wine glass.

"Grim was the same," adds Hadley. "But we're in Bertie's, and I'm pretty sure Albert and Arthur have us covered."

I glance over at the security spread around the edge of the room and give a smile. "I think we'll be perfectly safe here."

"So, that's two of you married off to the mafia," says Rylee.

"Living away from the club," adds Hadley, pouting.

"Hardly," says Meli, "I'm literally next door."

"And she's always in the clubhouse," Rylee points out. "We see her more now than when she lived with us."

Meli grins. "If you're complaining, I'll stay away, taking my babysitting duties with me."

Rylee laughs. "Don't you dare. You're a natural with Reuben."

"What about you?" asks Hadley, looking at me. "Will we be seeing you as much?"

I nod. "How will I annoy Dice if I'm not around?"

Astraea, Dice's ol' lady, laughs. "Don't let him fool you into thinking he doesn't miss you. His eyes light up whenever you're around to give him grief."

I smile. "How's he coping with baby Ivy?" I ask, feeling bad I haven't been around much to notice.

"He's a natural. Not that I ever doubted him," says Astraea. "She's got him wrapped around her little finger already."

"What's next for you and Albert?" asks Gracie.

I shrug. "I don't know. I never thought I'd be in this position, to be honest, so whatever happens next is a bonus."

"I must say, we were all very surprised to see you finally settling down," admits Rylee. "But we're so happy for you."

Meli flags a passing waitress to ask for a tray of shots. The rest of the group groan, knowing how crazy things can get once Meli starts bringing out the shots. When they arrive, she passes them out, missing her own. I raise a brow, and she smiles coyly. "I'll have to pass." We all turn our attention to her, and she holds up a glass of water. "I promised I wouldn't say. It's only eight weeks, but I can't keep it from you guys."

My mouth falls open in surprise. "Pregnant?" I whisper, and she nods enthusiastically.

"Oh my god," adds Hadley before throwing her arms around her sister. We all follow, congratulating her.

The others eventually go off to dance, leaving me alone with Meli. She takes my hand. "Are you okay? You seem quiet since I made the announcement."

"I'm just shocked," I reassure her. "I guess I . . ." I shake my head, trying to find the words.

"It passes," she says, tucking my hair away from my face. "The feeling that everything around you is going too well and it'll all come crashing down, it passes. You start to believe you're worthy enough to be loved."

I feel tears balancing on my lower lashes. "I keep pinching myself to check it's real. I don't know what he sees in me, Meli. Why does he want to take me and Ollie on?"

"Because you're fucking amazing, Rosey. It takes a good, strong man to handle you, and he does it with ease. He isn't going anywhere. You just have to let him love you."

I nod, knocking back another shot. "Do you mind if I sneak off?"

"Missing him already?" she asks, laughing.

I stand, kissing her on the cheek. "Something like that."

It's dark and the cab driver looks at me like I've lost my mind. "You sure, love? It's a bit secluded."

I pay him and get out. "I'll be fine. I'm a trained killer," I tell him, and he laughs before driving off.

I give the large metal gates a tug, but they're chained up. So, I grab the bars and haul myself up, throwing a leg over and climbing down the other side. My heels instantly sink into the soggy ground, but it doesn't deter me as I make my way to my destination.

I stare down at Eagle's headstone. The single red rose I brought here all those months ago is shrivelled and lifeless. "I assume you don't get to watch us from hell, and maybe that sort of thing is reserved for heaven." I crouch down. "I don't know why I'm here," I admit. "I think a part of me feels it's a good way to tie loose ends. You'd think I wouldn't need to after I put you down there in the first place. I'll be honest, Eagle, I've been freefalling through life since I was fucking born, and every damn day's been a fight. I joke around and hide all my insecurities behind my smart remarks and trigger-happy finger, but deep down, I'm a mess. But I guess you knew that already.

"I often think about what my life would have been if I was born into a good family with a mum and a dad, maybe some siblings. If I'd have had someone to guide me and show me how to live a normal life. And then I think of the good things I have, things I'd never have had if I'd been normal. I wouldn't have The Perished Riders, I wouldn't have Ollie, and I wouldn't have Albert. So, I guess I'm trying to say, I'm good with how things have worked out. I'm glad you gave me Ollie, and that I got to love him enough for the both of us. I'm glad he's got siblings who love him and will do anything for him, and now, he's got a dad. A good dad who'll treat him how a son should be treated."

I wipe my eyes, not realising I'd been crying until now. I give a small laugh and release a heavy breath. "I'm letting it all go, Eagle. The anger, the hurt, the pain. I'm gonna give normal a shot. Well, as normal as I can be. I'm gonna love my boy even harder, and I'm gonna let Albert love us both, in a way you never could have. So, goodbye, Eagle. From this moment on, I'll never think about you again."

As I walk past the church, I notice the door ajar, so I push my way in. Michael, the vicar and a club member, is sitting hunched over on the front pew. When he hears my footsteps, he stands, checking his watch. "Rosey, it's almost midnight, is everything okay?"

I nod. "Yeah. Can I light a candle?" He frowns but nods anyway. "I climbed the gates," I add as a way of explanation, and he laughs. I light the candle and say a silent goodbye to my mum. I hated that woman, but, fuck, I loved her too. "I'm marrying Albert Taylor," I tell Michael.

"That's fantastic news. Have you set the date?"

"I don't want it in here," I say, looking around the cold church. "Will you do it at the clubhouse?"

Michael nods. "Of course."

"I don't want all the big party and fuss. Just us, saying our vows."

"It's your big day, it's your choice."

"Can we do it today? Obviously, when it's daylight," I say, adding a nervous smile.

"Are you sure? These things usually take a little working out. I'm sure Albert can sort a licence, but you know I'd usually ask you to attend a few services and—"

ALBERT

"Michael, we both know I'm not a believer. If God was real, he would have taken me out by now. I just want to be Albert's wife. Make it happen. Please."

He gives a small laugh again and shakes his head. "Fine. I'll talk to Mav and make the arrangements. Let's say noon?"

I kiss him on the cheek. "Thank you."

Chapter Eighteen

ALBERT

I'm awoken with a painfully hard erection, and before I can register what's going on, Rosey is sinking down onto it. "Fuck," I groan. "Good night?"

"The best," she whispers, leaning down to kiss me.

I slip her bra straps down her shoulders and admire her perfect body as she rides me. "You're cold," I whisper, running my fingers down her chest and over her breasts.

"Marry me," she pants, moving faster.

"Name a day and time and I'll be there," I say, gripping her hips and thrusting up to chase my release.

She shudders, moaning as she comes. "Today at noon," she whispers, falling over my chest.

ALBERT

I spin us around so she's under me and continue to fuck her. "Are you drunk?"

"A little."

"We can't organise a wedding in a few hours, baby," I whisper, kissing her. I come hard, thrusting my release deep into her.

"I've got the vicar sorted," she says, smirking.

I frown. "You're serious?" She nods, and I laugh, burying my face in the crook of her neck and inhaling her scent. "You're crazy," I mutter, nipping her soft skin. "What's brought this on?"

"I love you," she says simply. "There's no one else for me, just you. If you'll have me?"

I pull her into my side and hold her. "I'm never letting you go."

Everyone looks at me like we've lost the plot. "We don't have time to question Rosey's state of mind right now," says Mav, grinning. "We have a wedding to organise."

"She doesn't want a fuss. Just some chairs so you can watch the service, and no wedding reception," I add.

"We're having a wedding reception," snaps Meli, and Arthur takes her hand.

"This isn't about us, baby. Rosey wants simple, do simple."

She scowls. "I don't know how."

I take Meli by the shoulders. "How about we set up the chairs outside and you go and find my beautiful bride-to-be and help her with hair and makeup?" She looks slightly more appeased as she heads off. I turn back to Arthur. "Right, organise the chairs, I need to head back to the house to speak to Ollie."

"Now you're my fucking boss?" he complains.

I grin. "It's my wedding day, give me some power."

Ollie is in the kitchen eating breakfast. "Meli is seriously moody today," he complains. "She practically screamed the house down for Mum a second ago. She woke me up."

I sit down. "Yeah, she's on one." I take a deep breath. "I need to ask you something."

"Again? You're always asking me stuff."

"This is huge . . . bigger than the house thing."

ALBERT

"Jesus, tell me she ain't pregnant. Would I have to share my room?"

I smirk. "No, she's not pregnant . . . yet. And no, there're other bedrooms. Your mum asked me something last night, and you know how she gets when she's got an idea." He eyes me suspiciously. "But her asking me isn't very traditional, so I wanted to do things properly, even though we're short on time. And she doesn't have a dad, so you're the man in her life—"

"Spit it out," he cuts in.

I laugh nervously. "I want to marry your mum. So, I'm asking you first."

He thinks for a few minutes. "And she's asked you already?" I nod. "Do you want to marry her? Would you still be asking if she hadn't asked first?"

"Ollie, I've wanted to ask her for months, but I thought she'd run a mile. I love her more than anything, and I promise I'll take care of her . . . of you both."

Ollie smiles. "I think I just threw up in my mouth," he jokes, and I playfully tap his head. "I told you, if she's happy, I'm happy. And I think it might be cool to have a dad." My heart swells, and we stare at each other. "Don't make it weird," he adds as a threat, and we both laugh.

"And if you're gonna be my dad, you have to do things right, like take me to football matches," he continues, "and give me an allowance."

I scoff. "For chores. Nothing's for free, kid."

He grins. "I'll do chores. Except babysitting. You two have more kids, you gotta look after them."

I nod, still smiling. "Deal. Now, let's go find you a suit."

ROSEY

I pace the room, occasionally catching a glimpse of the ivory material. I stop in front of the mirror again. The dress that Mama B presented me with just an hour ago made my heart stop. It's lace and fitted, with a beautiful long trail. Apparently, she'd made it herself years ago and stashed it away in her wardrobe, forgetting all about it. She said it was perfect for a last-minute wedding. "Don't you dare cry. I'm not redoing your eye makeup," warns Meli.

"It's just so beautiful. Why would she give it to me?"

"Look, I know you think the world hates you, but Mum loves you and Ollie. She feels guilt, massive amounts, for what Dad put you through, but don't mistake that for her not liking you because she does, a lot."

She sprays my hair one final time and turns me to face her. "For a last-minute wedding, I've done you proud."

I laugh at her self-praise. "Thank you, Meli. I love you."

Downstairs, Ollie is waiting in a blue suit. He looks handsome and it takes me a lot to hold back happy tears. "Well, don't you look amazing," I say.

"You don't look too bad yourself." He takes my hand and kisses me on the cheek. "Would you mind if I walked you down the aisle?"

"I'd love that, Ollie. I didn't think you'd want to."

"A chance to hand you over to someone else? Of course, I want to. It means he has to deal with you from now on."

I laugh, releasing his hand and hooking mine through his arm. "You better get me out there then."

The guys have done a wonderful job of setting out chairs. Flower petals have been sprinkled down the makeshift aisle and the seats are full of MC members and Taylors, all the people who matter to me the most. And at the front is Albert. He turns to face me as Meli presses play on her phone and Matt Johnson's "Feels Like Home" plays from the speakers. She'd insisted I pick a song to walk to and this was perfect.

As I get to the front, the song fades out and I give Ollie a kiss on the cheek. He steps away, and I turn to Albert. "Best-looking bride ever," he whispers.

Michael does his thing, and when it comes to exchanging vows, I stop him. "I'm not really for all that love, honour, and obey crap," I say. "Can we make up our own?"

"Go ahead," says Michael, looking exasperated. "Nothing else has been traditional."

Albert turns to Ollie, who hands him two wedding bands. I frown in confusion. "You won't believe the lengths we went to get these," Ollie tells me.

I turn back to Albert. "That's what I love the most," he says, taking my hands in his. "The fact you screw all the rules and do things your way. I never know what to expect, but you keep me on my toes. I promise to do all the stuff I'm supposed to, like take care of you, love you, cherish you, but I also promise to respect you, encourage you, and allow you to grow as that independent female you've always been. And on the days where you don't feel so independent, on the days you just need to lean on me, I'll be waiting. Because I love you, Rosey Taylor, with every

ALBERT

beat of my heart." I hear some of the women making 'aww' noises as he pushes the gold band onto my finger, then they clap.

I blow out a breath, not sure I have the right words, but his encouraging smile relaxes me. It's time to be real, to show everyone the real me. "Thank you," I say, staring into his eyes, "for being patient when you wanted to scream at me to listen. For loving me even when I wasn't very lovable. For caring when I needed it the most. I promise not to run anymore, not to push you away when deep down I just want to hold you close. I'll respect your role as my husband, even when I don't agree with what you're saying, and I'll try to listen more." He laughs at that one. "Because I love you, Albert Taylor, with every beat of my heart." I secure the ring onto his finger and smile.

Michael clears his throat. "All there is left to do is for you to kiss the bride." Cheers erupt as Albert takes me in his arms and kisses me until my toes curl. "I now pronounce you husband and wife. Mr. and Mrs. Taylor."

I turn towards everyone, and Albert holds our joined hands in the air. Everyone is smiling, including Ollie. And it suddenly hits me . . . I'm happy. This is what I was looking for all along and I didn't even know it. I finally have a family, something I've never really had. My life's about to change for the better, and I can't wait. I've found my happy ever after.

THE END

About the Author

I'm a UK author, based in Nottinghamshire. I live with my husband of many years, our two teenage boys and our four little dogs. I write MC and Mafia romance with plenty of drama and chaos. I also love to read similar books. Before I became a full-time author, I was a teaching assistant working in a primary school.

If you'd like to follow my writing journey, join my readers group on Facebook, which you'll find on the next page.

Social Media

You can visit my website where you'll find my latest projects, signed paperbacks and regular updates.
https://www.authornicolajane.com/

I love to hear from my readers and if you'd like to get in touch, you can find me here . . .

My Facebook Page

My Facebook Readers Group

Bookbub

Instagram

Goodreads

Amazon

Also By Nicola Jane

The Kings Reapers MC

Riggs' Ruin https://mybook.to/RiggsRuin

Capturing Cree https://mybook.to/CapturingCree

Wrapped in Chains https://mybook.to/WrappedinChains

Saving Blu https://mybook.to/SavingBlu

Riggs' Saviour https://mybook.to/RiggsSaviour

Taming Blade https://mybook.to/TamingBlade

Misleading Lake https://mybook.to/MisleadingLake

Surviving Storm https://mybook.to/SurvivingStorm

Ravens Place https://mybook.to/RavensPlace

NICOLA JANE

Playing Vinn https://mybook.to/PlayingVinn

The Perished Riders MC
Maverick https://mybook.to/Maverick-Perished
Scar https://mybook.to/Scar-Perished
Grim https://mybook.to/Grim-Perished
Ghost https://mybook.to/GhostBk4
Dice https://mybook.to/DiceBk5
Arthur https://mybook.to/ArthurNJ

The Hammers MC (Splintered Hearts Series)
Cooper https://mybook.to/CooperSHS
Kain https://mybook.to/Kain
Tanner https://mybook.to/TannerSH

Printed in Dunstable, United Kingdom